Contents

STAR

THE CLONE WARS

WARS

Pedigree

Published by Pedigree Books Ltd, Beech Hill House,
Walnut Gardens, Exeter, Devon EX4 4DH.
www.pedigreebooks.com • books@pedigreegroup.co.uk Published 2010.

£7.99

The treacherous Count Dooku, leader of the Separatists, has pledged his allegiance to the Sith Order. His instructions come directly from the shadowy Darth Sidious, but even Dooku has no idea who his Master really is.

THE STORY

The Clone Wars are still raging across the galaxy as

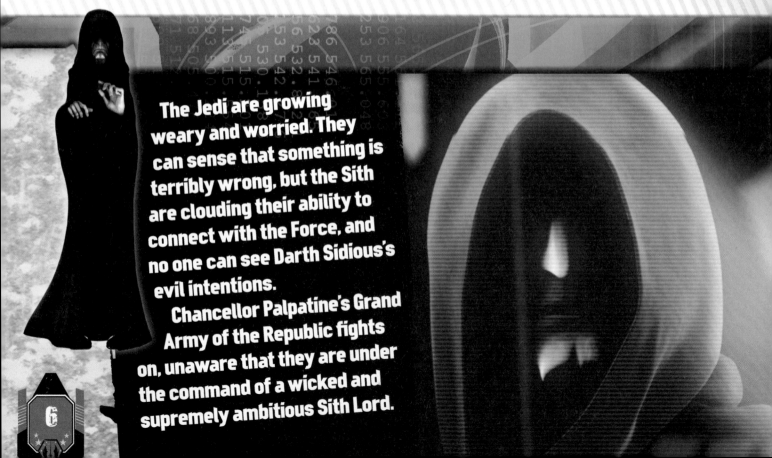

The Jedi are growing weary and worried. They can sense that something is terribly wrong, but the Sith are clouding their ability to connect with the Force, and no one can see Darth Sidious's evil intentions.

Chancellor Palpatine's Grand Army of the Republic fights on, unaware that they are under the command of a wicked and supremely ambitious Sith Lord.

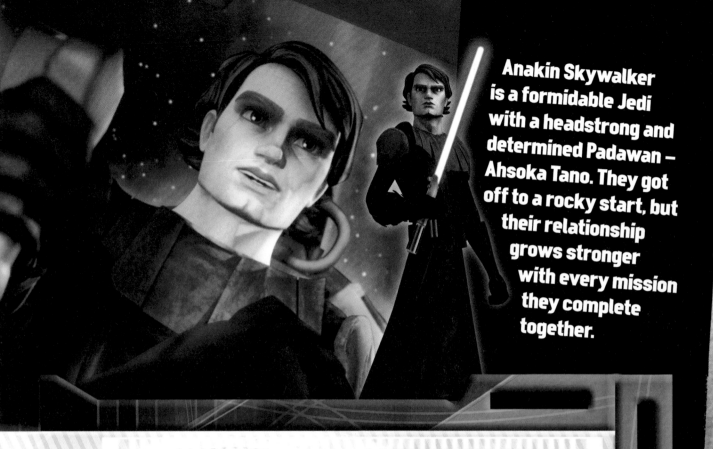

Anakin Skywalker is a formidable Jedi with a headstrong and determined Padawan – Ahsoka Tano. They got off to a rocky start, but their relationship grows stronger with every mission they complete together.

SO FAR....

the loyal Jedi fight to maintain democracy.

As they journey through the galaxy, missions and adventures fill every waking moment. They carry out the orders of the Jedi Council and defend the values of the Republic... but they also manage to have a bit of fun along the way!

Who's Who?

Ahsoka Tano

Young, determined and enthusiastic, Ahsoka is keen to prove herself to the Jedi and to her Master. She has picked up a little of Anakin's impulsive style, and her lightsaber skills are impressive. She has a strong connection to the Force and is also a talented pilot.

Anakin Skywalker

Bold, reckless and full of adventurous spirit, Anakin has become one of the best-known knights of the Jedi Order. He is brave and skilful, but sometimes his impulsive nature leads him into trouble. His passion for justice inspires his young Padawan, but sometimes he still causes his fellow Jedi concern.

Plo Koon

Plo is a wise and kind Jedi. He has a highly developed sense of justice, and a great deal of compassion for the weak and unfortunate. Although he is extremely polite, he is also exceedingly stubborn, and will not back down if he believes that he is in the right.

Obi-Wan Kenobi

This thoughtful, wise and kind Jedi Master has a dry sense of humour, which sustains him during the darkest times of war. He is a skilled pilot and a formidable warrior, but his negotiating skills are peerless. He often resolves disputes without any need for bloodshed. Over the years he has learned to be cautious and deeply patient.

Mace Windu

Mace has pride in his strength and skill as a Jedi warrior. However, he recognises this trait in himself, and works hard to control it. Although he has a sharp tongue, he is always ready to praise the achievements of others and quick to appreciate a joke.

Admiral Kilian

Kilian is a senior officer in the Republic Navy. He has traditional ideas about his role as Admiral, and admires dedication and honesty very highly. Kilian values skilled soldiers and would lay down his life for the sake of his duty.

Sugi

Sugi is a female Zabrak bounty hunter. Like all bounty hunters she places a high value on money. However, she is fair in her dealings, and will not back out of a job once she has accepted it.

Embo

Embo is a male Kyuzo bounty hunter who is part of Sugï's band. His large-rimmed hat can be used as a weapon or a shield, and his athletic abilities are a great asset to the team.

Hondo Ohnaka

The leader of the Weequay pirates was sold into slavery as a child, but managed to escape and form his pirate band. Although he is oily and immoral in many ways, there is a kind of honour in him. He admires bravery and loyalty, and his sense of humour enables him to take both success and failure light-heartedly.

Bossk

This Trandoshan bounty hunter is cruel and pitiless. As with all members of his species, he has sensitive eyes and can regenerate lost limbs. He is very greedy and has an obsessive personality, carrying in his heart only hatred and a desire for revenge on those who have humiliated him.

Castas

Castas is a lazy Klatoonian bounty hunter who is always on the lookout for a way to earn easy money. His quick temper, combined with his poor intellect, often lead him into trouble.

Fong Do

This hot-tempered Nautolan lives in the dark, seedy underworld of Coruscant. He is always interested in ways to make money, and isn't afraid of a fight.

THE CLONE WARS
BOUNTY HUNTERS

In the skies above the planet of Felucia, a Jedi shuttle popped out of hyperspace. Recently a series of medical stations had been established in orbit across the galaxy, but they were an easy target for Separatist attacks. The Felucia medical station had stopped making contact, and three Jedi had been sent to investigate...

'Where's the medical station?' asked Ahsoka Tano, one of the youngest Padawans in the Jedi Order. 'I don't see anything on my scanners.'

Suddenly a warning alarm went off. Several Separatist vulture droids were heading straight for the shuttle.

'I guess we know now what happened to the medical station,' said Obi-Wan Kenobi dryly.

A massive explosion rocked the ship, and Anakin battled with the controls, struggling to keep the craft pointing towards Felucia and avoid the enemy fire. Another lucky blast crippled the shuttle and it plunged downwards.

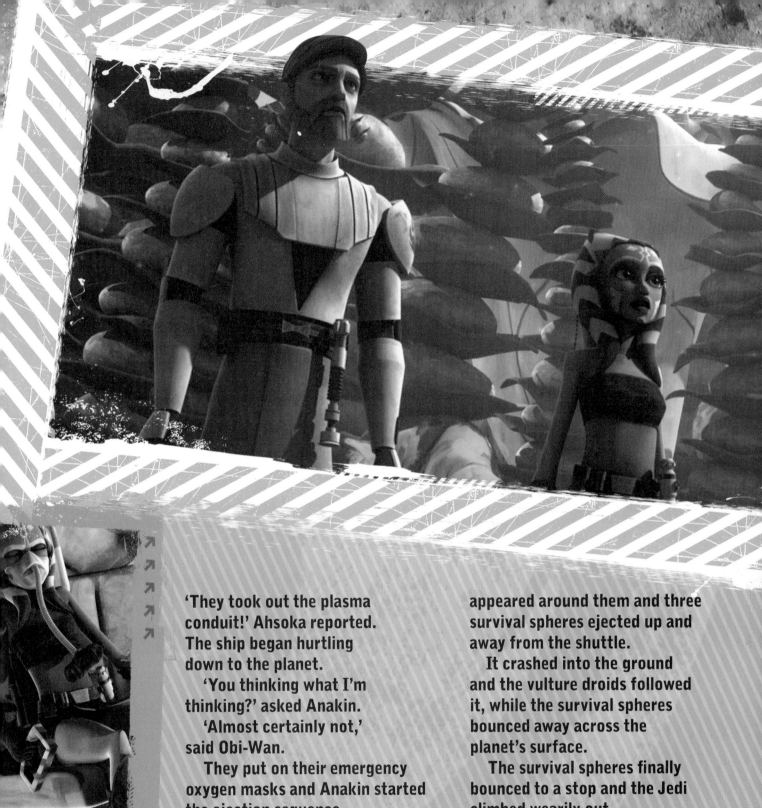

'They took out the plasma conduit!' Ahsoka reported. The ship began hurtling down to the planet.

'You thinking what I'm thinking?' asked Anakin.

'Almost certainly not,' said Obi-Wan.

They put on their emergency oxygen masks and Anakin started the ejection sequence.

'How come every time you fly, we crash?' Ahsoka enquired.

'It's not my fault,' said her Master. 'It's the ship.'

The three Jedi pulled their chair releases, safety capsules appeared around them and three survival spheres ejected up and away from the shuttle.

It crashed into the ground and the vulture droids followed it, while the survival spheres bounced away across the planet's surface.

The survival spheres finally bounced to a stop and the Jedi climbed wearily out.

They headed towards a small farming village that was visible on the horizon.

They found it was deserted, although the crops were in full bloom.

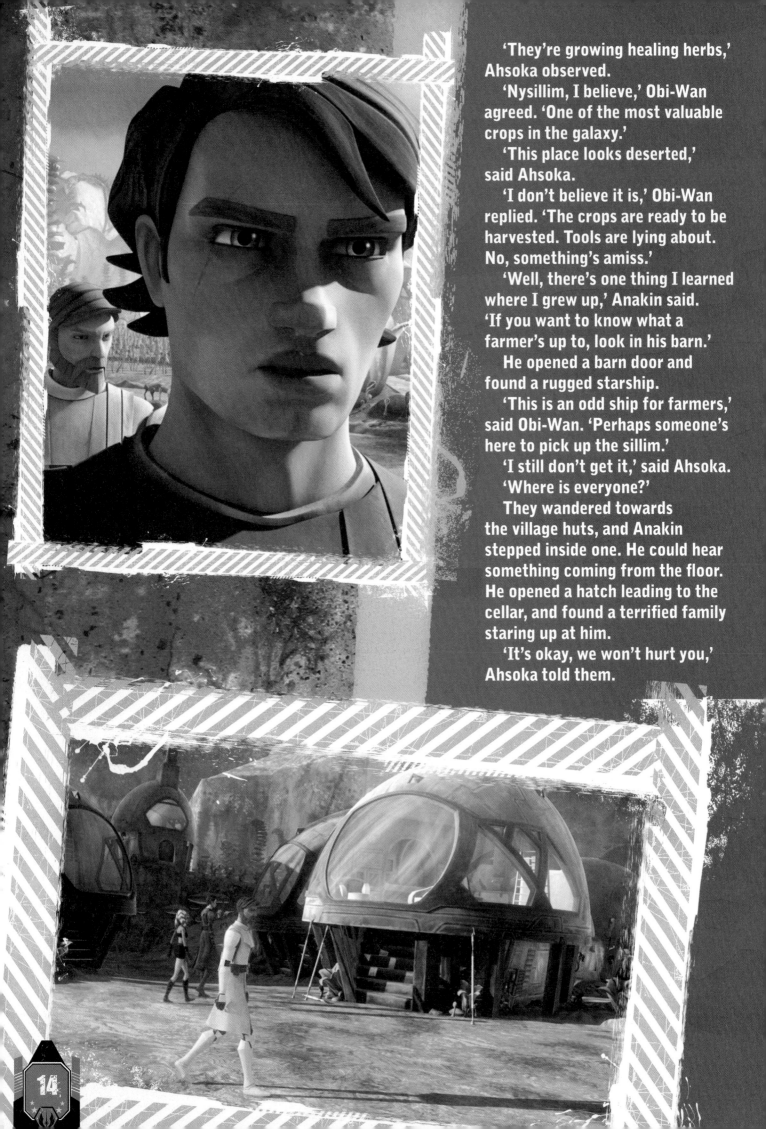

'They're growing healing herbs,' Ahsoka observed.

'Nysillim, I believe,' Obi-Wan agreed. 'One of the most valuable crops in the galaxy.'

'This place looks deserted,' said Ahsoka.

'I don't believe it is,' Obi-Wan replied. 'The crops are ready to be harvested. Tools are lying about. No, something's amiss.'

'Well, there's one thing I learned where I grew up,' Anakin said. 'If you want to know what a farmer's up to, look in his barn.'

He opened a barn door and found a rugged starship.

'This is an odd ship for farmers,' said Obi-Wan. 'Perhaps someone's here to pick up the sillim.'

'I still don't get it,' said Ahsoka. 'Where is everyone?'

They wandered towards the village huts, and Anakin stepped inside one. He could hear something coming from the floor. He opened a hatch leading to the cellar, and found a terrified family staring up at him.

'It's okay, we won't hurt you,' Ahsoka told them.

But as she spoke, a sound made them whirl around. Four bounty hunters were pointing their weapons at the Jedi. The leader spoke to them calmly.

'Kindly drop your weapons,' she said.

The Jedi stared at the bounty hunters. Sugi, the leader, was a Zabrak. A fearsome Kyuzo called Embo was carrying a heavy bowcaster.

There was also Rumi Paramita, a female Frenk with a rifle, and a bulky, armoured hulk called Seripas.

The bounty hunters were about to attack when a voice cried out, 'Stop! Don't harm them!'

The village elder, Casiss, raced into the hut.

'Can't you see these are Jedi?' he exclaimed. 'We are saved!'

'Need I remind you, Casiss,' said Sugi in a dangerous tone, 'you already made a deal with us?'

'But with the Jedi's help...'

'Help with what?' asked Ahsoka. Casiss looked grave.

'Pirates,' he said.

Later, inside his hut, Casiss explained the impossible position that they were in.

'If we don't give the pirates a portion of our crop, they will destroy our homes, with us in them,' he told them. 'Sillim farming is a meagre trade. Without our herbs to sell, we will have no money for food, fuel or equipment.'

'And yet you can afford to pay mercenaries?' asked the Jedi Master.

'These bounty hunters drive a far more reasonable bargain than the pirates,' said Casiss.

'Why not just fight them yourselves?' asked Anakin, always keen on action.

'Easy for you, perhaps,' Casiss replied. 'But look at us. We are farmers, not warriors.'

'What do you want, Jedi?' said Sugi.

'We need a ship,' said Obi-Wan. 'Ours is beyond repair, I'm afraid.'

'The one in the barn,' Anakin said, 'that'll do.'

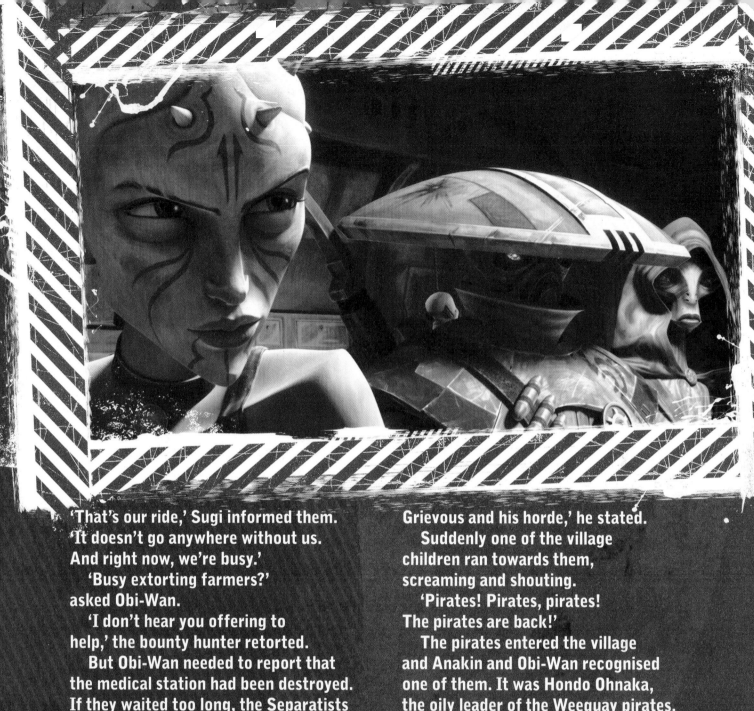

'That's our ride,' Sugi informed them. 'It doesn't go anywhere without us. And right now, we're busy.'

'Busy extorting farmers?' asked Obi-Wan.

'I don't hear you offering to help,' the bounty hunter retorted.

But Obi-Wan needed to report that the medical station had been destroyed. If they waited too long, the Separatists would come looking for them.

'Better they get robbed by pirates than attract the interest of General Grievous and his horde,' he stated.

Suddenly one of the village children ran towards them, screaming and shouting.

'Pirates! Pirates, pirates! The pirates are back!'

The pirates entered the village and Anakin and Obi-Wan recognised one of them. It was Hondo Ohnaka, the oily leader of the Weequay pirates.

The Jedi had already faced them once before on Florrum. What were they doing here?

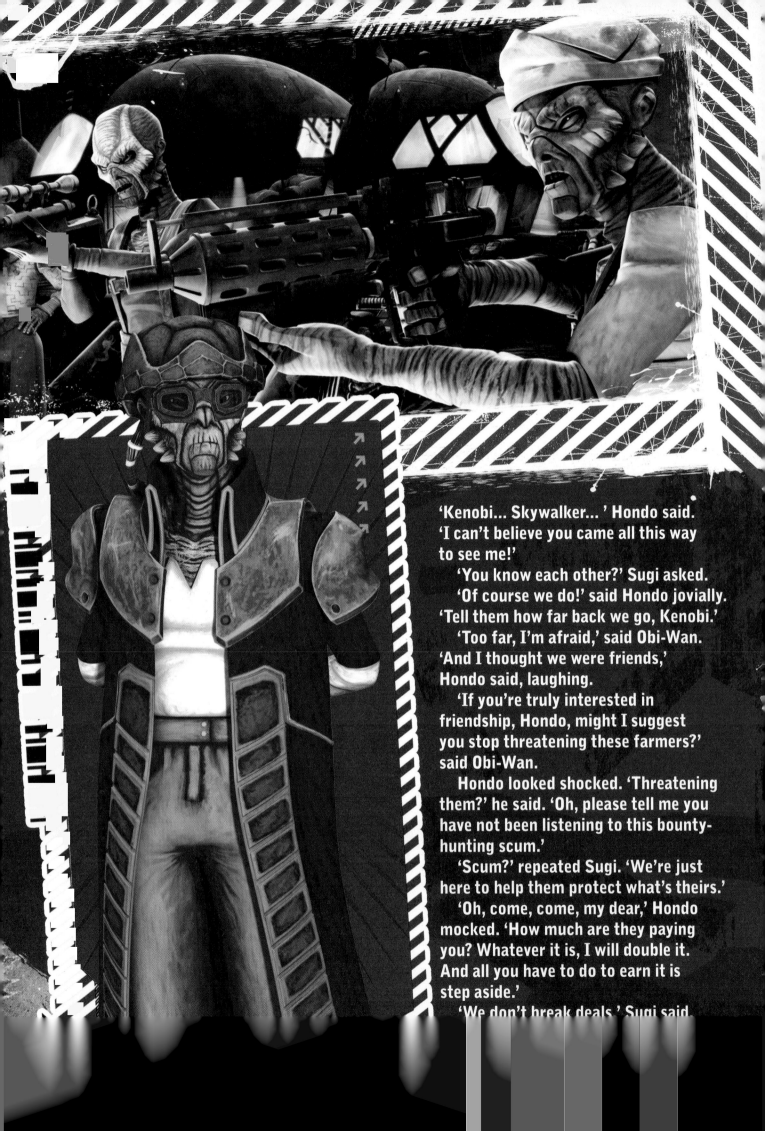

'Kenobi... Skywalker... ' Hondo said. 'I can't believe you came all this way to see me!'

'You know each other?' Sugi asked.

'Of course we do!' said Hondo jovially. 'Tell them how far back we go, Kenobi.'

'Too far, I'm afraid,' said Obi-Wan. 'And I thought we were friends,' Hondo said, laughing.

'If you're truly interested in friendship, Hondo, might I suggest you stop threatening these farmers?' said Obi-Wan.

Hondo looked shocked. 'Threatening them?' he said. 'Oh, please tell me you have not been listening to this bounty-hunting scum.'

'Scum?' repeated Sugi. 'We're just here to help them protect what's theirs.'

'Oh, come, come, my dear,' Hondo mocked. 'How much are they paying you? Whatever it is, I will double it. And all you have to do to earn it is step aside.'

'We don't break deals,' Sugi said.

Things were getting ugly. The bounty hunters and pirates drew their weapons.

'Steady, everyone,' said Obi-Wan, who was hoping to find a way to resolve things peacefully.

'All we want is a ride to the nearest Republic outpost. And I'm willing to pay you handsomely for it. Twice what you could make selling this crop.'

'Well now,' mused Hondo. 'How do plan to pay me?'

'A funds transfer when we arrive,' said Obi-Wan.

'Republic credit?' Hondo scoffed. 'We've been over this before, Kenobi. My associates don't accept that currency.'

'I'm offering a deal that benefits us all, Hondo,' Obi-Wan said. 'Don't let your greed blind you to that fact.'

'You know I like you, Kenobi,' said Hondo. 'But no one leaves this planet until I get my sillim.'

'Then, I hope you enjoy it here,' snapped Sugi, 'because you'll be staying a long time, parasite!'

'You know this crop has not been harvested,' said Hondo, glaring at Casiss. 'You'd better hurry, old man, before things start to die on you.'

The pirate shot Sugi and Obi-Wan a dirty look and walked away.

A short time later, inside a village hut, Obi-Wan was preparing to advise the Felucians and the bounty hunters. He had been studying the tactical layout of the village.

'When the attack comes, it will come from two fronts,' he said, showing everyone a hologram of the surrounding terrain. 'The forest to the south, and the ridge to the north. Whatever you do, you must defend both sides.

'But there are only four of them,' said one of the village farmers. 'How can four bounty hunters defend against so many?'

Anakin pulled Obi-Wan aside.

'The farmers are right,' he said in a low voice. 'These bounty hunters don't stand a chance.'

'We've been over this, Anakin,' said Obi-Wan.

'You seem to lack confidence in our abilities, young Jedi,' Sugi broke in.

'I'm sure you're good at what you do,' Anakin replied, 'but you are in way too deep.'

'Said the peace-keeper who fails t o keep the peace,' Sugi mocked.

'The rift in the galaxy is not our fault,' said Obi-Wan in a calm voice. 'If more worlds would stand up for themselves against the Separatists, this war would have been over long ago.'

Anakin's eyes suddenly began to gleam. He had an idea.

'That's it!' he exclaimed. 'We'll just train the villagers to defend themselves!'

Next morning, the Felucians used their hover combines to harvest the nysillin. Riding Tee-Musses, they pulled their bales to the barn. Meanwhile, Anakin and his Padawan were busy instructing a disorganised group of villagers.

They were clumsy and slow, but they were willing to try. Anakin showed them how to use pole-arms, while Ahsoka helped others master the slingshot.

Obi-Wan and Sugi walked through the barn as the bales were brought in.

'What happens if you need the barn as a fallback position?' Obi-Wan asked. 'With all the sillim here, it will be difficult to squeeze the farmers in.'

'There's room,' said Sugi in a brusque tone. 'I know what I'm doing and I will keep these people safe... my way.'

Ahsoka had noticed the well-armoured Seripas nearby.
He was using a saw to cut into the forest's pod-like trees.
As one began to topple, Seripas supported its weight himself.
   'Seripas!' Ahsoka cried. 'It's too heavy!'
She rushed to help him and shoved him to the ground, just
as the tree crashed down where he had been standing.
   'Seripas?' said Ahsoka, looking down at him.
There was something odd about the way his armour was moving.
Ahsoka drew closer, and then a small, frail alien popped out from
inside the armour. He looked horrified to have been seen by Ahsoka.
   'Don't look!' he cried. I'm... I'm having a suit malfunction.
Not very intimidating, am I?'
   Ahsoka smiled kindly.
'You don't have to look tough to be tough,' she said
as Seripas closed up his suit.
   'I thank you for your help,' he said.

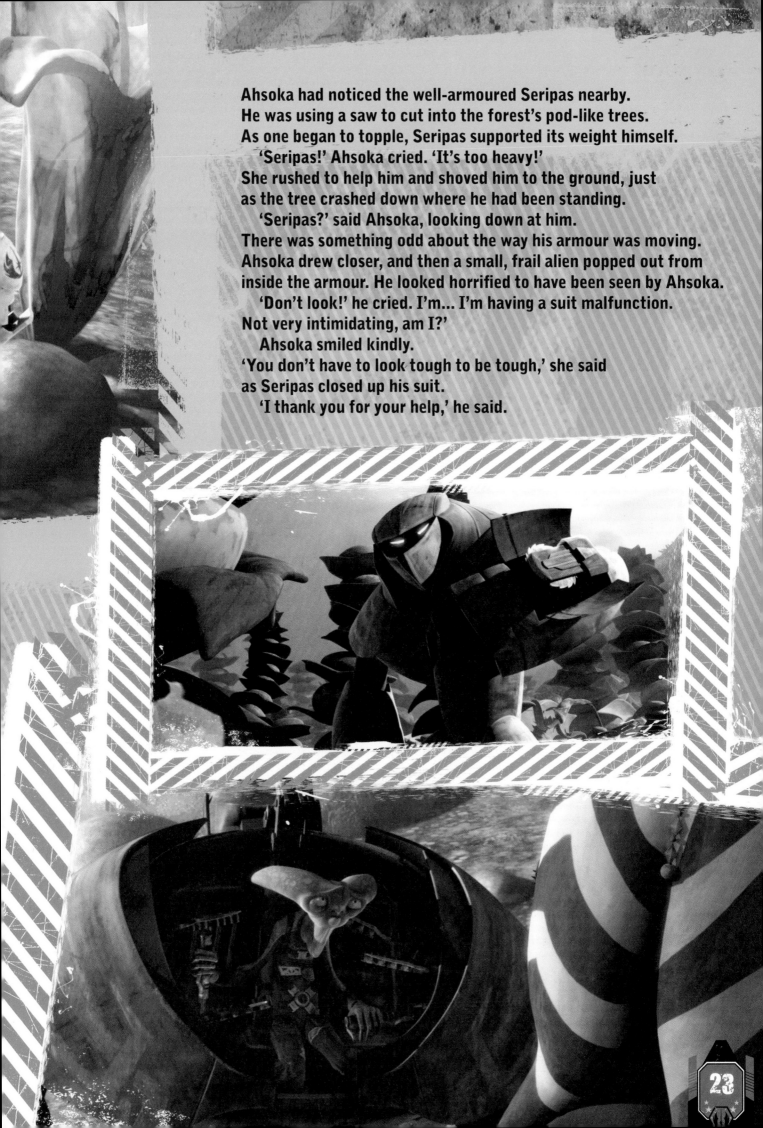

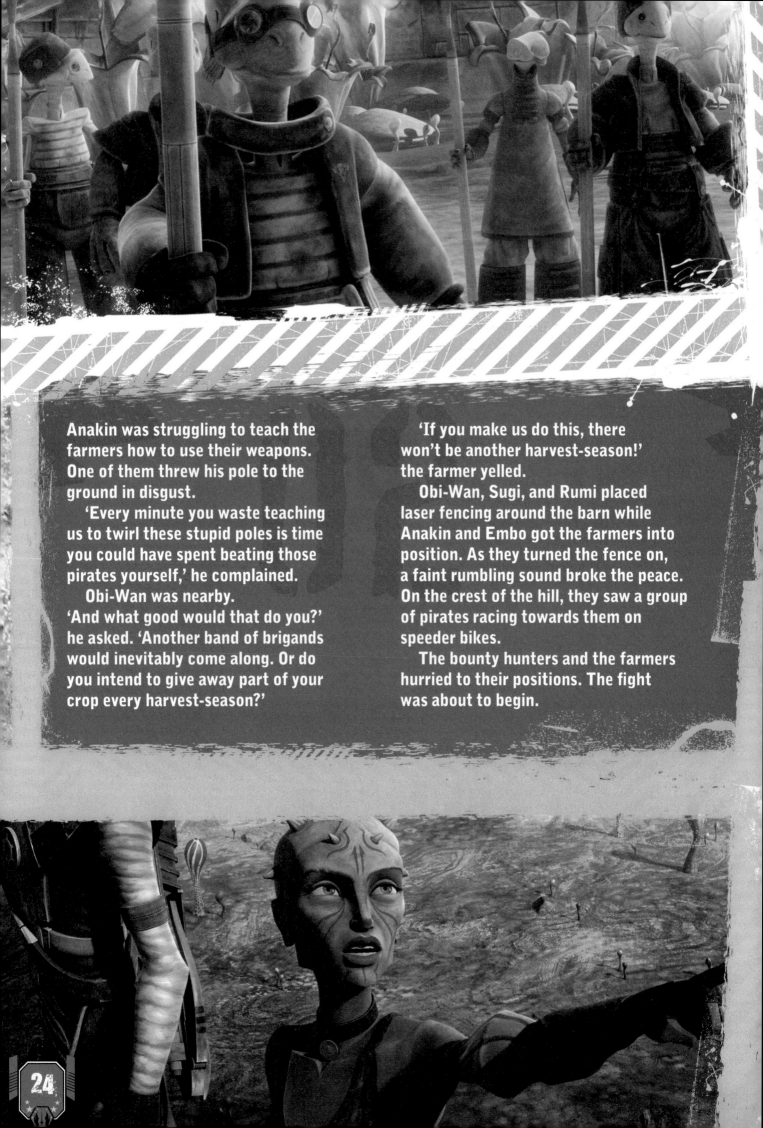

Anakin was struggling to teach the farmers how to use their weapons. One of them threw his pole to the ground in disgust.

'Every minute you waste teaching us to twirl these stupid poles is time you could have spent beating those pirates yourself,' he complained.

Obi-Wan was nearby.

'And what good would that do you?' he asked. 'Another band of brigands would inevitably come along. Or do you intend to give away part of your crop every harvest-season?'

'If you make us do this, there won't be another harvest-season!' the farmer yelled.

Obi-Wan, Sugi, and Rumi placed laser fencing around the barn while Anakin and Embo got the farmers into position. As they turned the fence on, a faint rumbling sound broke the peace. On the crest of the hill, they saw a group of pirates racing towards them on speeder bikes.

The bounty hunters and the farmers hurried to their positions. The fight was about to begin.

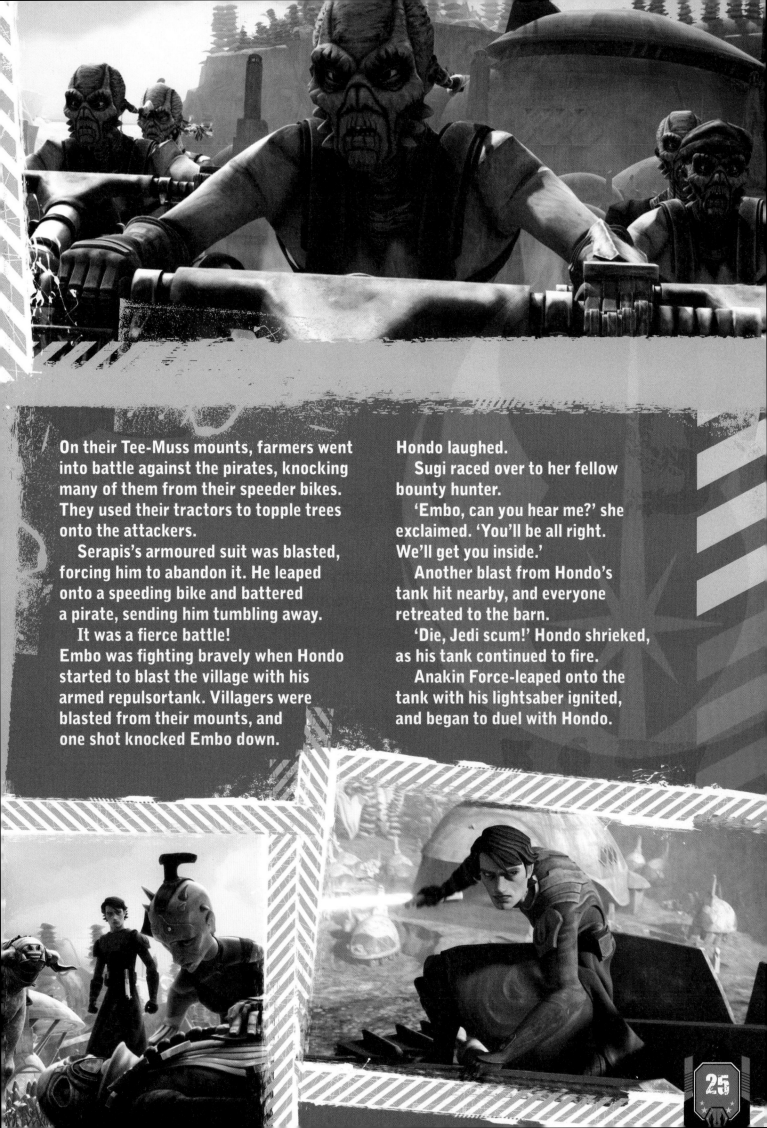

On their Tee-Muss mounts, farmers went into battle against the pirates, knocking many of them from their speeder bikes. They used their tractors to topple trees onto the attackers.

Serapis's armoured suit was blasted, forcing him to abandon it. He leaped onto a speeding bike and battered a pirate, sending him tumbling away.

It was a fierce battle! Embo was fighting bravely when Hondo started to blast the village with his armed repulsortank. Villagers were blasted from their mounts, and one shot knocked Embo down.

Hondo laughed.

Sugi raced over to her fellow bounty hunter.

'Embo, can you hear me?' she exclaimed. 'You'll be all right. We'll get you inside.'

Another blast from Hondo's tank hit nearby, and everyone retreated to the barn.

'Die, Jedi scum!' Hondo shrieked, as his tank continued to fire.

Anakin Force-leaped onto the tank with his lightsaber ignited, and began to duel with Hondo.

The bounty hunter Rumi was picking off pirates with her rifle when a blast from the tank hit her. She was killed instantly.

'No!' screamed Sugi.

But this was no time for mourning.

'Watch your flank!' Obi-Wan yelled. He used the Force to crash a pirate speeder into the laser fence and Sugi blasted them.

After a fierce duel, Anakin flipped Hondo over the edge of a cliff. Hondo teetered at the edge of the cliff in terror. When the pirates saw him there, they retreated and left the village.

'The day is won!' Casiss cried in triumph.

'Help me!' Hondo cried.

Anakin reached out his hand and pulled Hondo up, not realising that the tank was still moving behind him. Just as Hondo reached safety, he shoved Anakin towards the firing tank, which blasted the cliff away. Anakin leaped out of the way and landed in the village below.

'This effort is no longer profitable,' Hondo muttered.

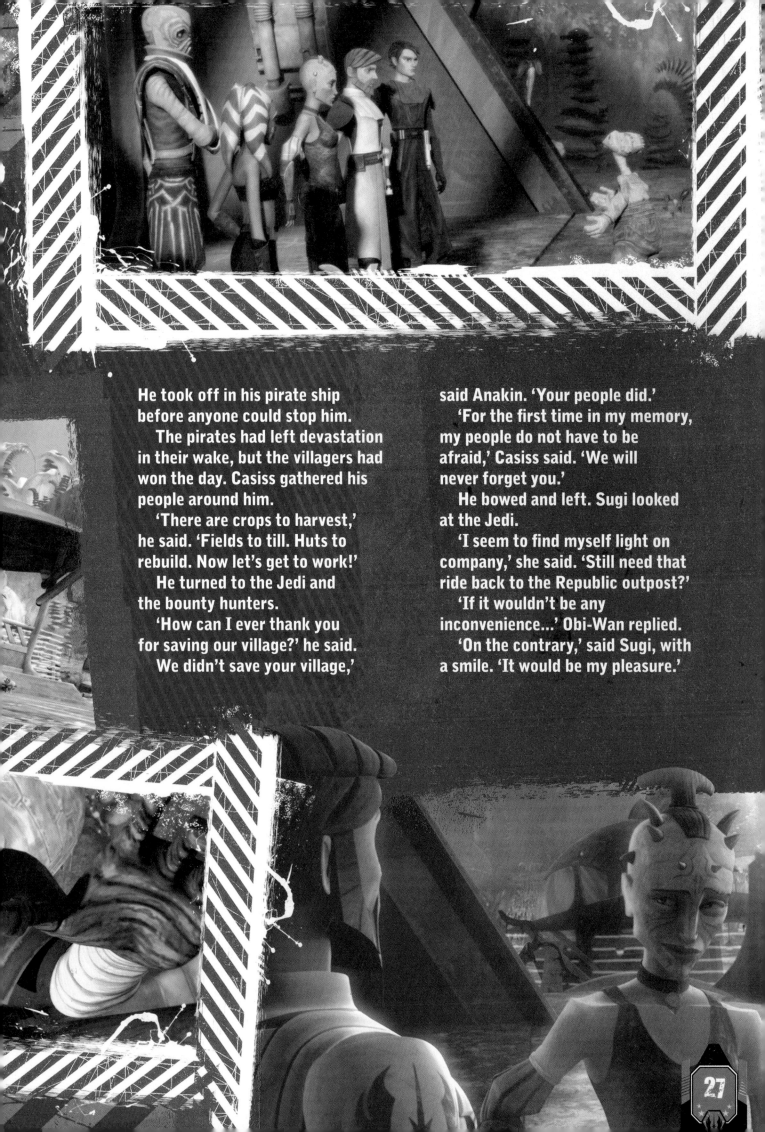

He took off in his pirate ship before anyone could stop him.

The pirates had left devastation in their wake, but the villagers had won the day. Casiss gathered his people around him.

'There are crops to harvest,' he said. 'Fields to till. Huts to rebuild. Now let's get to work!'

He turned to the Jedi and the bounty hunters.

'How can I ever thank you for saving our village?' he said.

We didn't save your village,' said Anakin. 'Your people did.'

'For the first time in my memory, my people do not have to be afraid,' Casiss said. 'We will never forget you.'

He bowed and left. Sugi looked at the Jedi.

'I seem to find myself light on company,' she said. 'Still need that ride back to the Republic outpost?'

'If it wouldn't be any inconvenience...' Obi-Wan replied.

'On the contrary,' said Sugi, with a smile. 'It would be my pleasure.'

Rancor Risk

Obi-Wan, Anakin and Ahsoka have landed on an unfamiliar planet. There are jungle rancors all around them. Guide them to the safety of the farming village without bumping into any of the dangerous beasts.

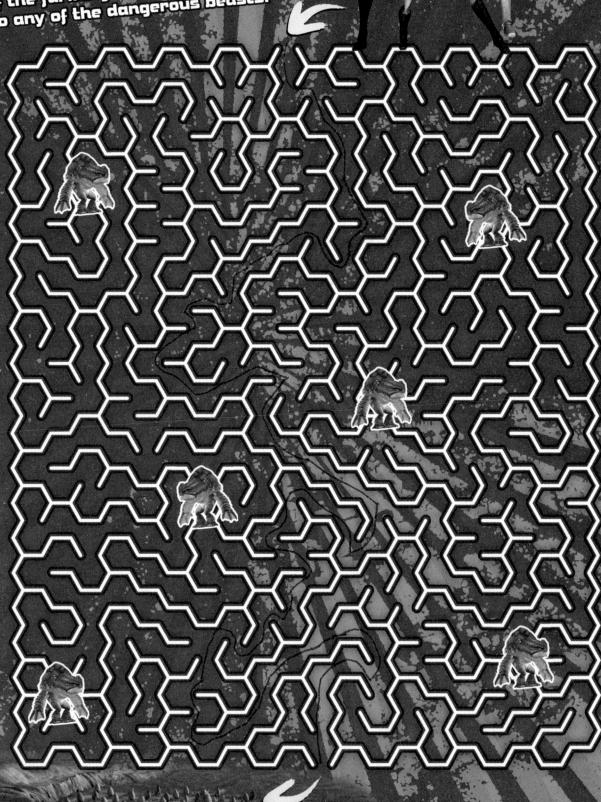

Clone in Hiding

**One of these clone cadets is Boba Fett.
Can you identify the odd one out? Draw a circle
around the cadet that you think is Boba Fett.**

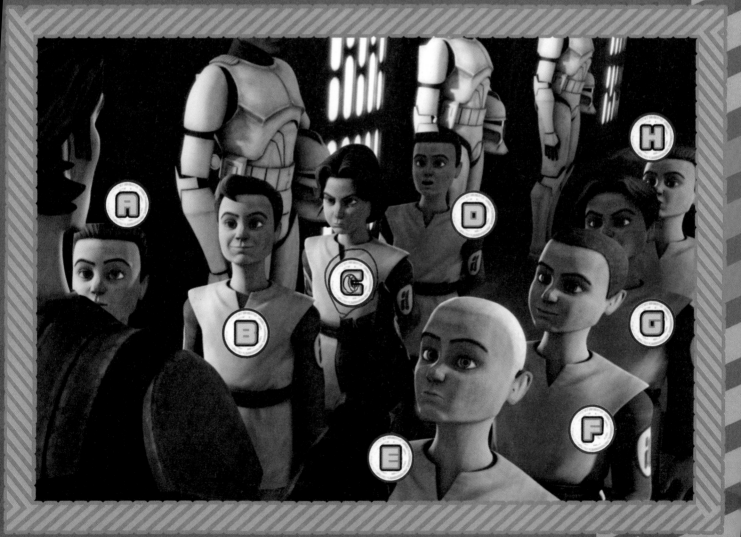

29

HOW TO DRAW Boba Fett

Follow these step-by-step instructions and learn how to draw Jango Fett's vengeful son.

1 Draw pencil lines to mark out the position of Boba's body, arms and legs. Use circles to show his hands and knee joints, and lines to show the angle of his weapons.

2 Draw a rough outline of Boba's body shape and clothing.

Fill in the detail of his clothing, face and weapons.

Add shading and finer details, rubbing out the rough pencil lines as you go.

Connections

All these sentences have something in common. Each one is missing two names! The second name in each sentence is the first name in the following sentence. Using your knowledge of Jedi adventures, can you work out what these unfinished sentences say? (The first sentence has been completed to get you started.)

① **Padmé Amidala is secretly married to** Anakin Skywalker.

② Anakin Skywalker **was once** Obi-Wan Kenobi **'s Padawan.**

③ Obi-Wan Kenobi **sits on the Jedi Council with** Mace Windu **, who has a purple lightsaber.**

④ Mace Windu **killed** Jango Fett **at the Battle of Geonosis.**

⑤ Jango Fett **was the father of** Boba Fett

⑥ Boba Fett **travels the galaxy with a female bounty hunter called** Aurra Sing

Sudoku

Sharpen your mind power with this challenging puzzle. Each row and column must include numbers 1 to 9 in any order. Also, each small 3 by 3 square must include numbers 1 to 9.

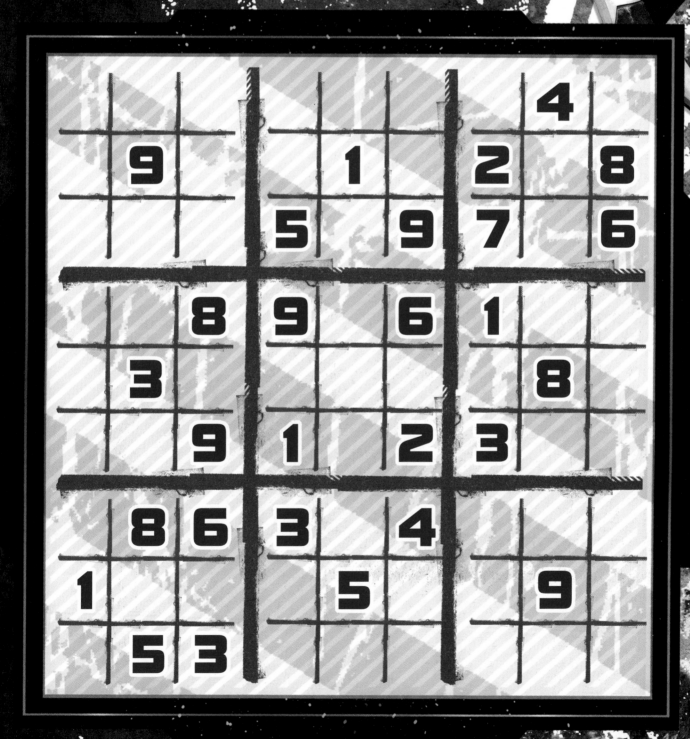

Padmé's Guide to Diplomacy

As a Senator, I know how important diplomacy can be. It is vital to know how to say the right things to the right people. Being unaware of personal tensions or intergalactic disagreements could lead to conflict and war. Here are my tips to help you develop your diplomatic skills.

What is Tact?

Being tactful is being considerate of the feelings and opinions of other people. If you have to make an unpopular decision or tell someone something they don't want to hear, it's tactful to speak the truth with kindness and thoughtfulness.

What is Diplomacy?

It's the art of managing situations and discussions so that both sides are happy with the outcome. That might be between friends, groups, countries or planets. Diplomacy also means standing up for yourself and your opinions without having an argument.

No Means No

Be decisive when your answer is no. Politely explain why you are refusing, but don't be too apologetic.

Body Language

- Keep eye contact with the other people.
- Sit upright and relax your hands and shoulders.
- Don't hold your breath
- Do not whisper or raise your voice.
- Practise a plain, pleasant facial expression in the mirror.

Show Respect

Accept that other people have viewpoints that are different from yours. Respect their needs and feelings, just as you want them to respect yours.

Team Effort

Don't think of this as an argument. Think of it as a team effort to solve a problem.

Listen

Listen to what people say. You can sometimes summarise their points to let them know you understand their views. If you don't understand, ask questions.

Interruptions

Don't interrupt other people when they are talking. If someone interrupts you, politely ask him or her to allow you to finish your thought. Encourage them to make their point after you've finished.

Be Language Clever

Use peaceful phrases like 'I think' or 'It seems as if' instead of attacking phrases like 'You always' and 'You never'. Use simple language and speak clearly to make sure that you can be understood.

Forget Feelings

Focus on the facts of the matter. Opinions are for the mind and diplomacy is for the mouth!

Dealing with arguments

Sometimes people just seem to want to have an argument. If they will not calm down, try these suggestions:
- Try to steer the conversation back to the original point.
- Remember that the other person might have issues that you don't know about yet.
- Don't take criticism to heart.
- If things get heated, have a five-minute break to allow everyone to calm down.
- Tell them that you will discuss the subject again at another time, then leave.

Scrambled Words

What famous names are hidden in these scrambled sentences?

1. Soak an oath

2. On a hand hook

3. Bet of bat

4. Sugar rain

5. Acts as

6. Weak onion bib

JEDI CHALLENGE

EXERCISE YOUR LOGIC WITH THESE PUZZLING RIDDLES. CAN YOU SOLVE THEM ALL?

1 Whoever makes it doesn't want it. Whoever takes it doesn't know about it. Whoever knows about it doesn't want it.
What is it?

2 I am weightless, but the strongest person in the galaxy can't hold me for much more than a minute.
What am I?

3 I can run but can't walk, have a mouth but can't talk, have a head but can't weep, have a bed but don't sleep.
What am I?

4 You can see me, but I am weightless. You can put me in a bucket and I'll make it lighter.
What am I?

5 I went into the forest and got it. I sat down to look for it. I brought it home because I couldn't find it.
What is it?

6 What can you catch but not throw?

THE CLONE WARS
DEATH TRAP

The Jedi Cruiser *Endurance* was preparing to meet a Republic frigate. The frigate was carrying a class of clone cadets, who were eager to explore the warship. Just before the frigate docked, the Clone sergeant addressed the boys.

'You have the best training in the galaxy, but no one can train you for the moment you look death in the eyes,' he said. 'What you do then, and the soldier you become – that is up to you.' He dismissed them, and the clone cadets relaxed. Two of them, Whiplash and Hotshot, noticed a new boy standing by himself. He looked somehow different, which was weird. All the clones looked alike – that was the point.

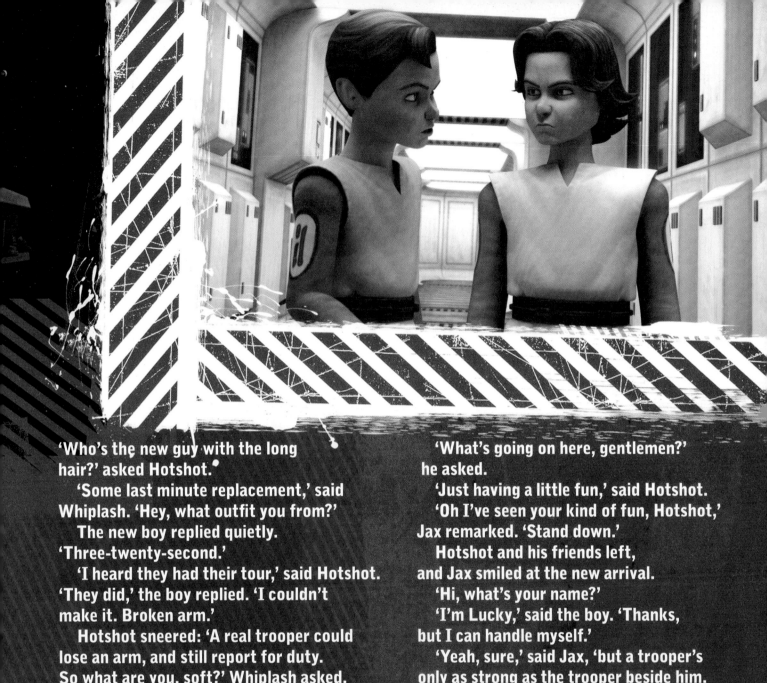

'Who's the new guy with the long hair?' asked Hotshot.

'Some last minute replacement,' said Whiplash. 'Hey, what outfit you from?'

The new boy replied quietly. 'Three-twenty-second.'

'I heard they had their tour,' said Hotshot.

'They did,' the boy replied. 'I couldn't make it. Broken arm.'

Hotshot sneered: 'A real trooper could lose an arm, and still report for duty. So what are you, soft?' Whiplash asked.

Another cadet, Jax, noticed what was happening.

'What's going on here, gentlemen?' he asked.

'Just having a little fun,' said Hotshot.

'Oh I've seen your kind of fun, Hotshot,' Jax remarked. 'Stand down.'

Hotshot and his friends left, and Jax smiled at the new arrival.

'Hi, what's your name?'

'I'm Lucky,' said the boy. 'Thanks, but I can handle myself.'

'Yeah, sure,' said Jax, 'but a trooper's only as strong as the trooper beside him. We're all in it together, right?'

Lucky gave a small smile. 'Right.'

The frigate docked with the cruiser and the cadets disembarked in neat military rows. A row of clone troopers was waiting to greet them.

Almost all the cadets stared eagerly at their older counterparts. Only Lucky turned his eyes away, as if he could not bear to look.

'Don't be nervous,' said Jax. 'Only thing between us and them is experience. It's not like they're Jedi.'

At that moment the doors whooshed open and two Jedi strode in – Anakin Skywalker and Mace Windu.

'Welcome aboard the Jedi cruiser *Endurance*,' said Mace. 'I am Mace Windu. And this is…'

'Anakin Skywalker, welcome aboard,' said Anakin. 'Today, you'll see how a real, working Jedi cruiser operates. And you'll have the chance to serve right alongside two Jedi Knights.'

But as the cadets chattered excitedly, the Jedi were called away to a meeting in the War Room. Lucky watched them go with a fierce intensity.

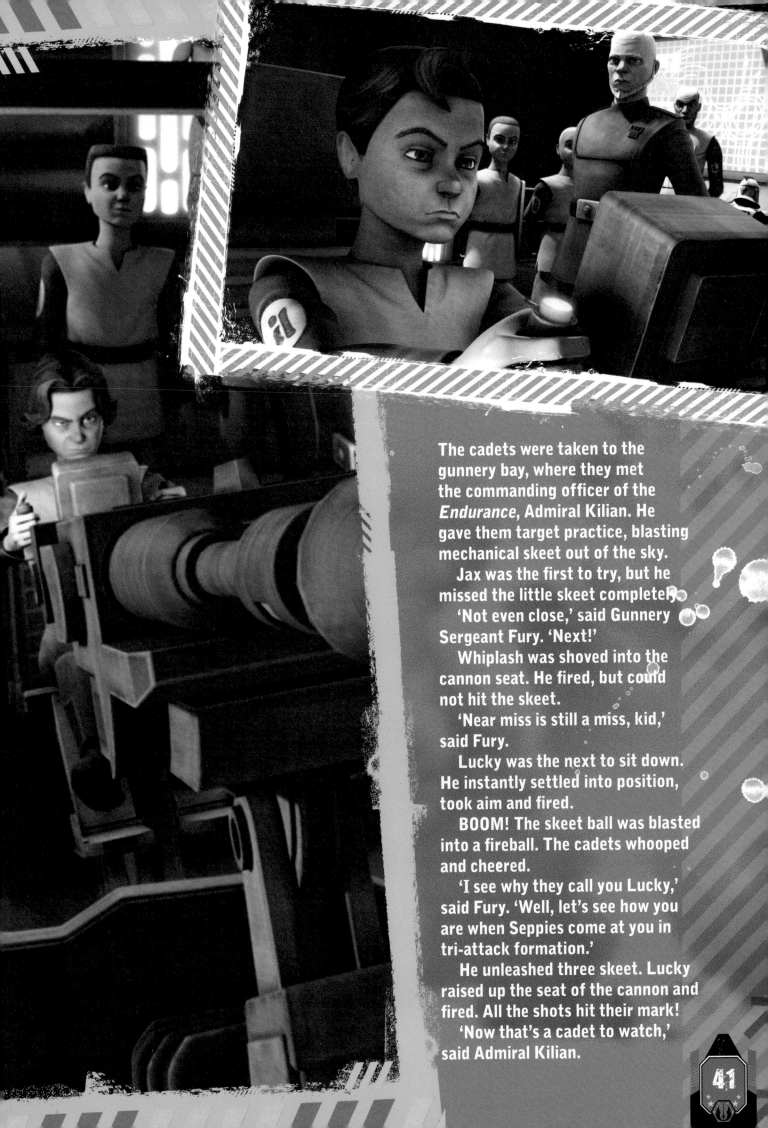

The cadets were taken to the gunnery bay, where they met the commanding officer of the *Endurance*, Admiral Kilian. He gave them target practice, blasting mechanical skeet out of the sky.

Jax was the first to try, but he missed the little skeet completely.

'Not even close,' said Gunnery Sergeant Fury. 'Next!'

Whiplash was shoved into the cannon seat. He fired, but could not hit the skeet.

'Near miss is still a miss, kid,' said Fury.

Lucky was the next to sit down. He instantly settled into position, took aim and fired.

BOOM! The skeet ball was blasted into a fireball. The cadets whooped and cheered.

'I see why they call you Lucky,' said Fury. 'Well, let's see how you are when Seppies come at you in tri-attack formation.'

He unleashed three skeet. Lucky raised up the seat of the cannon and fired. All the shots hit their mark!

'Now that's a cadet to watch,' said Admiral Kilian.

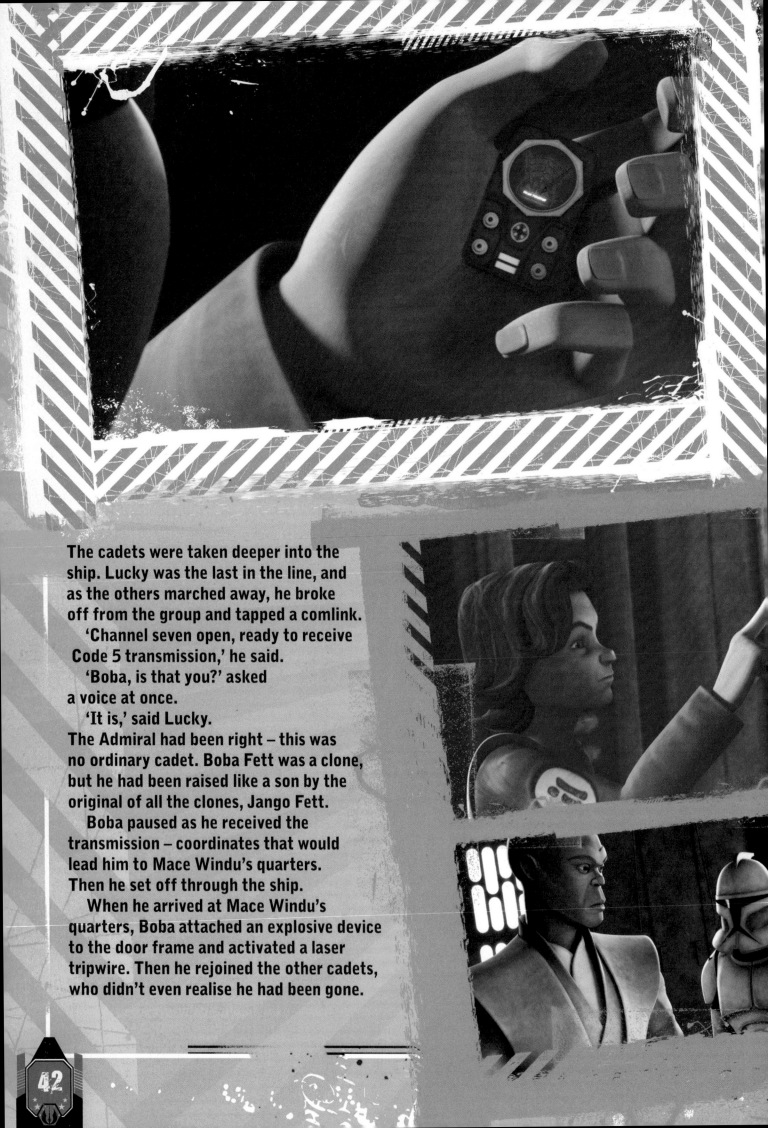

The cadets were taken deeper into the ship. Lucky was the last in the line, and as the others marched away, he broke off from the group and tapped a comlink.

'Channel seven open, ready to receive Code 5 transmission,' he said.

'Boba, is that you?' asked a voice at once.

'It is,' said Lucky.
The Admiral had been right – this was no ordinary cadet. Boba Fett was a clone, but he had been raised like a son by the original of all the clones, Jango Fett.

Boba paused as he received the transmission – coordinates that would lead him to Mace Windu's quarters. Then he set off through the ship.

When he arrived at Mace Windu's quarters, Boba attached an explosive device to the door frame and activated a laser tripwire. Then he rejoined the other cadets, who didn't even realise he had been gone.

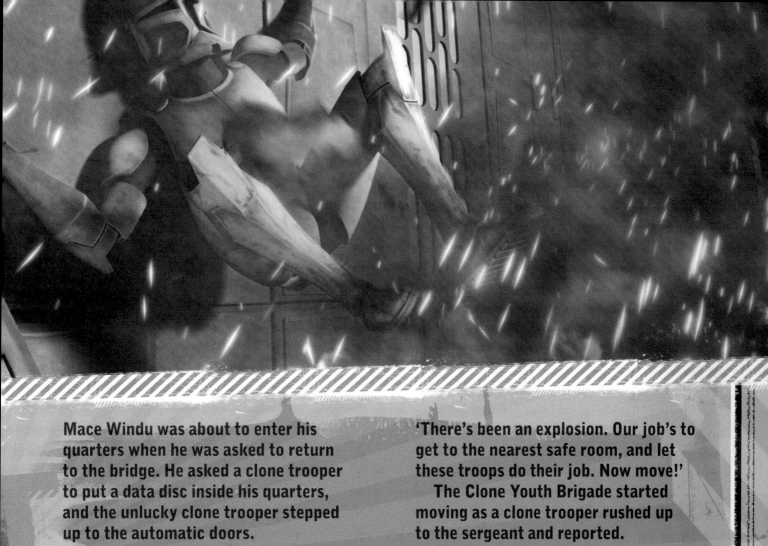

Mace Windu was about to enter his quarters when he was asked to return to the bridge. He asked a clone trooper to put a data disc inside his quarters, and the unlucky clone trooper stepped up to the automatic doors.

BOOM! His body flew backwards and alarms rang out around the ship.

In one of the corridors, the cadets stared as clone troops raced past.

'This doesn't look like a drill,' said Jax to Boba.

'No time for chatter,' said their sergeant.

'There's been an explosion. Our job's to get to the nearest safe room, and let these troops do their job. Now move!'

The Clone Youth Brigade started moving as a clone trooper rushed up to the sergeant and reported.

'Ship's undamaged, one man down,' he said. 'General Windu's quarters got hit but he survived.'

'Survived?' muttered Boba Fett in disappointment.

He slipped away from the group as they marched steadily on.

Mace Windu could tell that this was no accident. Knowing that the ship's navigation was located close to his quarters, Mace made contact with Admiral Kilian on his comlink.

'Admiral, has the navigation been damaged?' he asked.

'Hobbled, not destroyed,' replied the Admiral's voice.

'Systems are reparable. I've ordered shutdown of all engines until we're fully operational. We'll hold orbit over Vanqor.'

Anakin looked at Mace with concern in his eyes.

'If navigation wasn't the target, then hitting your quarters was intentional,' he said.

Anakin and Mace gave orders to search the ship for the assassin.

Meanwhile, Boba had made contact with his accomplice.

'It's a miss, repeat miss,' he reported. 'What should I do?'

'Head to the reactor, blow the core,' came the instruction.

'But the crew... ' said Boba in an uncertain voice. 'It isn't about them, just Mace.'

'If you want Windu dead, do as I say!' snapped his accomplice.

Boba entered the main reactor room and came face to face with a clone trooper. It was still hard for him to look at them. They were exact copies of his father – who Mace Windu had beheaded at the start of the Clone Wars.

Boba missed his father with an aching, gnawing pain that never seemed to go away.

Boba told the clone trooper that he was lost. As the trooper turned away to request an escort for the cadet, Boba took his blaster and hit him on the head. The blow glanced off the trooper's helmet.

'What?' exclaimed the trooper. Boba hit him again, knocking his helmet off.

'What are you doing?' cried the trooper. 'We're brothers! Don't shoot!'

'You're not my brother,' said Boba. He shot the trooper with a stun blast. Then he blasted the reactor's control panel and fired on the reactors.

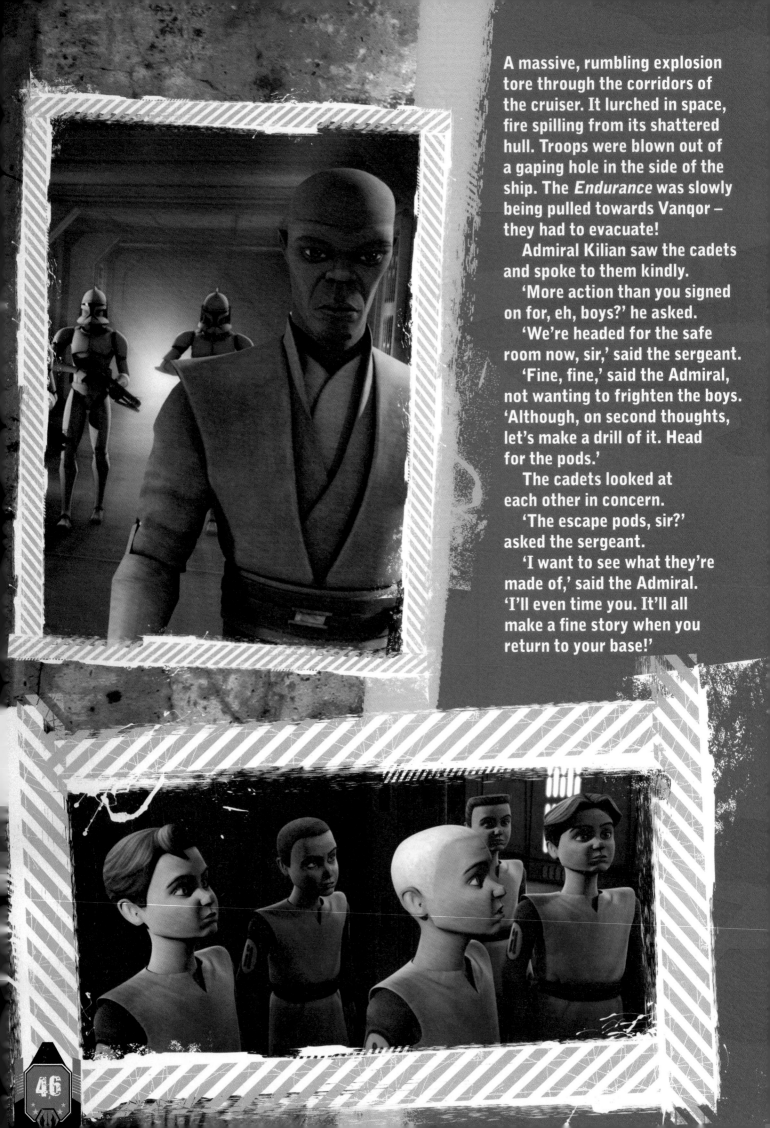

A massive, rumbling explosion tore through the corridors of the cruiser. It lurched in space, fire spilling from its shattered hull. Troops were blown out of a gaping hole in the side of the ship. The *Endurance* was slowly being pulled towards Vanqor – they had to evacuate!

Admiral Kilian saw the cadets and spoke to them kindly.

'More action than you signed on for, eh, boys?' he asked.

'We're headed for the safe room now, sir,' said the sergeant.

'Fine, fine,' said the Admiral, not wanting to frighten the boys. 'Although, on second thoughts, let's make a drill of it. Head for the pods.'

The cadets looked at each other in concern.

'The escape pods, sir?' asked the sergeant.

'I want to see what they're made of,' said the Admiral. 'I'll even time you. It'll all make a fine story when you return to your base!'

Boba was running through the ship when a hand reached out and grabbed him. It was the clone sergeant.

'Lucky, stay with the group!' he ordered.

'Yes sir,' said Boba, rejoining the other cadets.

'How we gonna get through this?' asked Whiplash.

'Groups of four, men,' the sergeant ordered. 'Take pods one and two. Set rendezvous coordinates with the other pods, at a safe distance from the cruiser.'

He ushered the cadets to a row of escape pods and they climbed in. One by one, the escape pods were jettisoned into space.

Boba found himself sharing a pod with Jax, Hotshot and Whiplash. As soon as he could do it without being seen, he sabotaged the air brakes. Jax desperately tried to steer as the pod spun out of control.

'The pod's malfunctioned!' he cried. 'We missed the rendezvous!' exclaimed Hotshot as they passed the other escape pods.

'I can't stop it!' Jax yelled.

Anakin and Mace returned to the bridge of the ship.

'The main reactor's beyond hope,' said Anakin. 'You have to abandon ship.'

'No,' said the Admiral unexpectedly. 'You must abandon ship. I'm staying.'

Anakin and Mace exchanged a look. They had not realised that Kilian had such traditional ideas.

'Admiral, you must abandon ship,' said Mace.

'Not a chance,' the Admiral replied.

'But sir,' said Anakin, 'with respect, that's an order.'

Kilian did not move. 'It may be your command, General, but we don't have time for that kind of sentiment!' Anakin erupted.

'It's not sentiment,' said Kilian. 'An Admiral must go down with his ship. I don't expect you to understand it, Jedi.'

The Jedi could not make him change his mind. Several of his men also wanted to stay behind. Anakin and Mace had to leave without them.

The Jedi climbed into their ships to leave the cruiser, together with R2-D2 and the clone troops. Once they were outside, they turned to look at the situation.

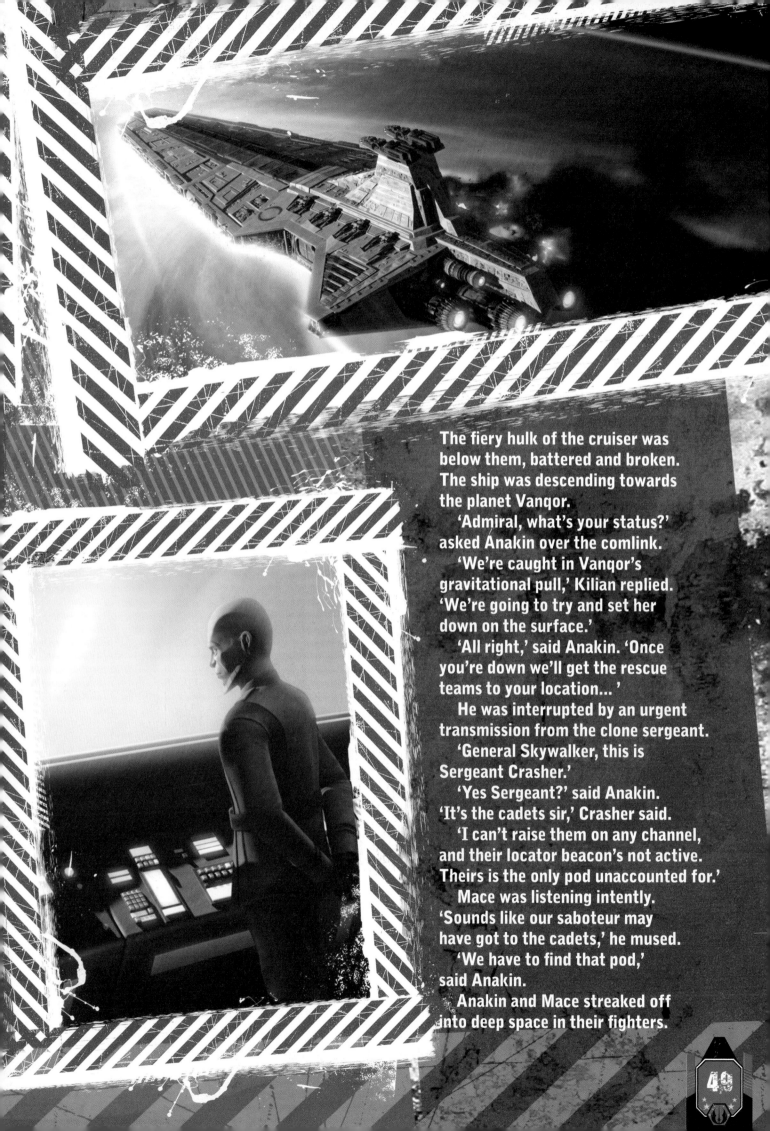

The fiery hulk of the cruiser was below them, battered and broken. The ship was descending towards the planet Vanqor.

'Admiral, what's your status?' asked Anakin over the comlink.

'We're caught in Vanqor's gravitational pull,' Kilian replied. 'We're going to try and set her down on the surface.'

'All right,' said Anakin. 'Once you're down we'll get the rescue teams to your location... '

He was interrupted by an urgent transmission from the clone sergeant.

'General Skywalker, this is Sergeant Crasher.'

'Yes Sergeant?' said Anakin. 'It's the cadets sir,' Crasher said.

'I can't raise them on any channel, and their locator beacon's not active. Theirs is the only pod unaccounted for.'

Mace was listening intently. 'Sounds like our saboteur may have got to the cadets,' he mused.

'We have to find that pod,' said Anakin.

Anakin and Mace streaked off into deep space in their fighters.

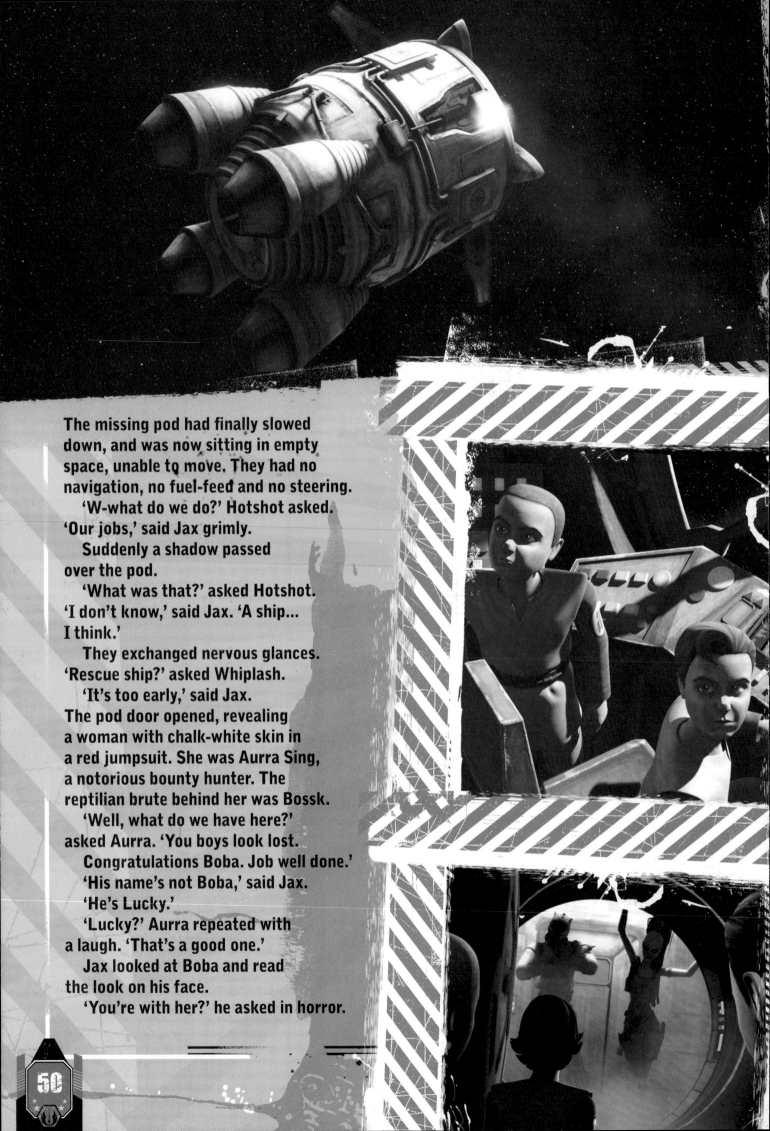

The missing pod had finally slowed down, and was now sitting in empty space, unable to move. They had no navigation, no fuel-feed and no steering.

'W-what do we do?' Hotshot asked.
'Our jobs,' said Jax grimly.

Suddenly a shadow passed over the pod.

'What was that?' asked Hotshot.
'I don't know,' said Jax. 'A ship... I think.'

They exchanged nervous glances.
'Rescue ship?' asked Whiplash.

'It's too early,' said Jax. The pod door opened, revealing a woman with chalk-white skin in a red jumpsuit. She was Aurra Sing, a notorious bounty hunter. The reptilian brute behind her was Bossk.

'Well, what do we have here?' asked Aurra. 'You boys look lost. Congratulations Boba. Job well done.'

'His name's not Boba,' said Jax. 'He's Lucky.'

'Lucky?' Aurra repeated with a laugh. 'That's a good one.'

Jax looked at Boba and read the look on his face.

'You're with her?' he asked in horror.

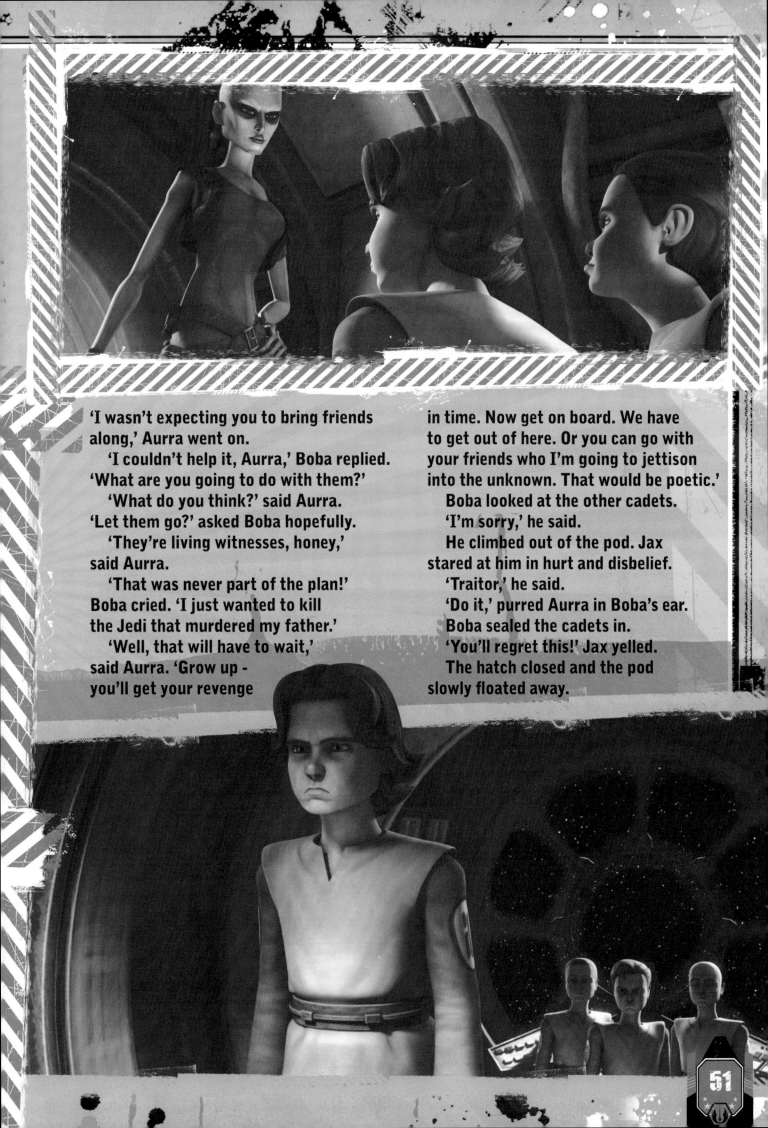

'I wasn't expecting you to bring friends along,' Aurra went on.

'I couldn't help it, Aurra,' Boba replied. 'What are you going to do with them?'

'What do you think?' said Aurra.

'Let them go?' asked Boba hopefully.

'They're living witnesses, honey,' said Aurra.

'That was never part of the plan!' Boba cried. 'I just wanted to kill the Jedi that murdered my father.'

'Well, that will have to wait,' said Aurra. 'Grow up - you'll get your revenge in time. Now get on board. We have to get out of here. Or you can go with your friends who I'm going to jettison into the unknown. That would be poetic.'

Boba looked at the other cadets.

'I'm sorry,' he said.

He climbed out of the pod. Jax stared at him in hurt and disbelief.

'Traitor,' he said.

'Do it,' purred Aurra in Boba's ear.

Boba sealed the cadets in.

'You'll regret this!' Jax yelled.

The hatch closed and the pod slowly floated away.

The cadets worked frantically on the pod controls.

'I can't believe it,' Hotshot muttered. 'A traitor, he was a traitor.'

'We can't worry about that right now,' said Jax. 'We have to find a way to contact somebody.'

'We already tried!' Hotshot exclaimed. 'This pod is dead – we only have minimal life support.'

'Well whose fault is that?' Whiplash added, glaring at Jax. 'None of us. That guy you defended left us for dead!'

'Stow it, Whiplash,' said Jax. 'We need to work together.'

But Whiplash was working himself up into a fury.

'You're not in charge here!' he shouted.

For a moment it looked as if he might hit Jax, but then a bright light entered the pod, blinding them.

'They've come back to finish us off!' Hotshot wailed.

'No!' cried Jax, looking out of the window. 'It's the Jedi!'

Outside, Mace and Anakin's Jedi starfighters were floating near the pod. The cadets knew that they were going to be all right.

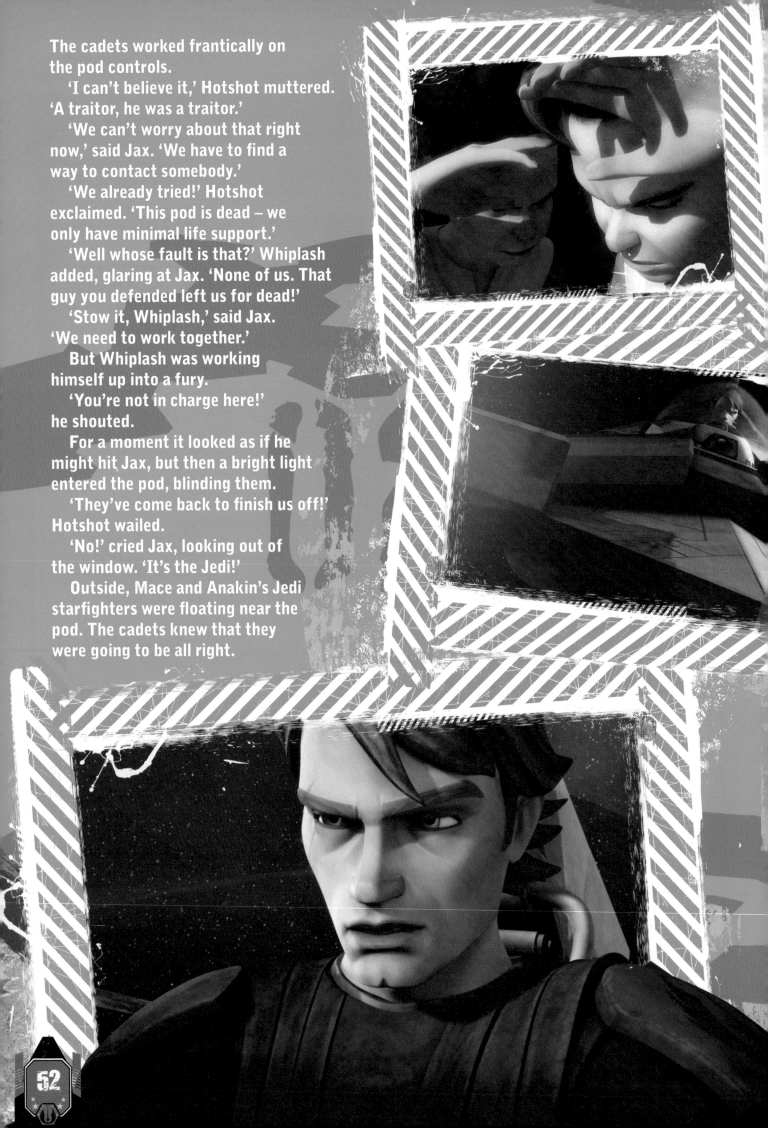

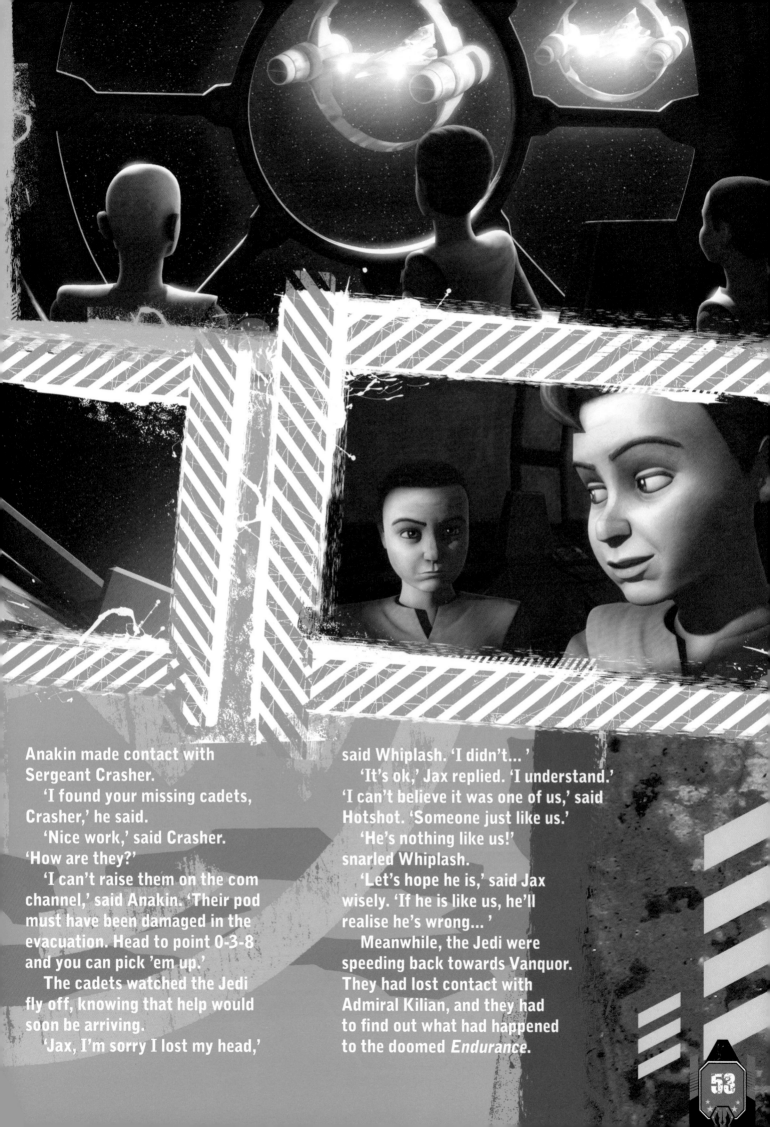

Anakin made contact with Sergeant Crasher.

'I found your missing cadets, Crasher,' he said.

'Nice work,' said Crasher. 'How are they?'

'I can't raise them on the com channel,' said Anakin. 'Their pod must have been damaged in the evacuation. Head to point 0-3-8 and you can pick 'em up.'

The cadets watched the Jedi fly off, knowing that help would soon be arriving.

'Jax, I'm sorry I lost my head,' said Whiplash. 'I didn't... '

'It's ok,' Jax replied. 'I understand.'

'I can't believe it was one of us,' said Hotshot. 'Someone just like us.'

'He's nothing like us!' snarled Whiplash.

'Let's hope he is,' said Jax wisely. 'If he is like us, he'll realise he's wrong...'

Meanwhile, the Jedi were speeding back towards Vanquor. They had lost contact with Admiral Kilian, and they had to find out what had happened to the doomed *Endurance*.

BOARD GAME

Start

01

02

03

YOUR WORK ON THE ENGINES KEEPS THEM GOING. HAVE ANOTHER TURN.

BOBA FETT HAS SABOTAGED THE JEDI CRUISER ENDURANCE, AND TIME IS RUNNING OUT. CAN YOU PILOT THE SHIP SAFELY TO THE SURFACE OF THE PLANET BEFORE THE ENGINES FAIL?

05

06

09

07

BOBA FETT KNOCKS YOU OUT. MISS A TURN.

10

YOU GET LOST IN THE SHIP'S CORRIDORS. GO BACK FIVE SPACES.

11

YOU REFUSE TO ABANDON SHIP. GO FORWARD TWO SPACES.

13

14

16

32

31

30

34

35

Finish

ADMIRAL KILIAN PROMOTES YOU. GO FORWARD THREE SPACES.

YOU ARE CAUGHT IN AN EXPLOSION AND HAVE TO BE CHECKED BY A MEDICAL DROID. GO BACK TWO SPACES.

YOU EVACUATE THE CADETS SAFELY. GO FORWARD BY THE NUMBER OF PEOPLE PLAYING THE GAME.

25

24

27

28

23

YOU WILL NEED A DICE, COUNTERS AND A FEW FRIENDS TO PLAY AGAINST. THE FIRST PLAYER TO REACH THE SURFACE OF VANQOR IS THE WINNER.

YOU FALL ASLEEP ON DUTY. MISS A TURN.

17

ANAKIN SKYWALKER PRAISES YOUR PILOTING SKILLS. HAVE ANOTHER TURN.

20

21

19

55

Grid Drawing

COPY THIS PICTURE OF BRAVE DROID R2-D2. USE THE GRIDLINES TO HELP YOU MAKE A PERFECT COPY. THEN COLOUR IN YOUR PICTURE.

Coded Message

Anakin and Obi-Wan often write to each other in a code that only they can understand. Use their secret code to write a letter to your best friend. Copy the decoder for them on a separate piece of paper. Then see how long it takes your friend to decode the message.

A → *
B → 3
C → .
D → +
E → 5
F → /
G → 7
H → =
I → 9
J → !
K → @
L → 1
M → ^
N → &
O → 8
P → ?
Q → <
R → ~
S → 6
T → >
U → "
V → 4
W → %
X → $
Y → ¥
Z → £

SOLAR SYSTEM

If you were able to design and plan a solar system, what would it be like? Use this area to imagine your own magnificent creation. How many suns will your system have? How many planets? What size and colour will they be, and what will you call them?

WHEN YOU HAVE DRAWN AND COLOURED IN THE SUNS, PLANETS AND MOONS OF YOUR NEW SYSTEM, LABEL EACH ONE WITH A NAME AND A DESCRIPTION. THERE IS NO LIMIT TO WHAT YOU CAN ACHIEVE!

THE CLONE WARS
R2 COME HOME

Following the unexpected explosion on board the Jedi cruiser *Endurance*, a Republic medical frigate was busily gathering the scattered escape pods. Mace Windu and Anakin Skywalker plunged their starfighters into the planet Vanqor 's atmosphere.

The *Endurance* had crashed, carving an enormous furrow into Vanqor's crystalline landscape. Debris was scattered for miles around. The cruiser was a smouldering wreck, but the bridge looked mostly intact.

'Let's hope Admiral Kilian and the command crew are still in one piece,' said Mace. 'Set down behind the cruiser, we'll approach on foot.'

They landed their starfighters away from the shaky wreckage and made their way towards it on foot. Their astromech droids accompanied them – R2-D2 with Anakin and R8-B7 with Mace.

'You're not kidding, little buddy,' said Anakin, looking around. 'I don't like the feel of this place either.'

'Your astromech is programmed to feel?' asked Mace in surprise.

'Artoo is kind of a special case,' said Anakin.

Mace looked dubious. 'He's got a lot of personality, that's all,' said Anakin.

'You encourage it too much,' Mace remarked.

They walked on, looking around at the huge chunks of debris smoking all around. The ground was scorched and littered with burning pieces of wreckage.

'Ar-eight, start scanning the area for signs of life,' Mace ordered. 'And calculate an entry point to the cruiser.

R2-D2 beeped at Anakin.

'You're right Artoo, it doesn't look good,' agreed Anakin.

'A bit jittery, isn't it?' asked Mace. But Anakin knew his droid. 'He must have seen something, right Artoo?'

R2-D2 chirped a 'maybe'.

'Come on,' said Mace, 'it looks like R8 has found an entry point.'

Anakin glared at R2-D2, not wanting Mace to think his droid wasn't up to his job. They moved closer to the downed cruiser. But as they walked away, a pair of menacing eyes watched them go.

Mace, Anakin and R2-D2 stood just inside the jagged hole in the cruiser's hull, allowing their eyes to adjust to the darkness. R8-B7 shone his light into the hull. Wind-blown turquoise sand covered everything.

Not wishing to be outdone, R2-D2 turned his light on and scanned the interior. Then he let out a sad chirrup. His light had picked out the body of a clone. Mace rolled the body over and found a blaster bolt mark in its ches.

'This man did not die in the crash,' he said. 'He was executed, shot at close range.

'The killer?' Anakin asked. 'He beat us to the crash site? But why come here?'

'We know the assassins were after me,' said Mace. 'Perhaps they returned to look for my body?'

R2-D2 found another dead clone, who had died in the same way.

'We need to get to the bridge to find Admiral Kilian,' said Mace. 'Send the droids to scan for any survivors down here. Maybe the killer missed one.'

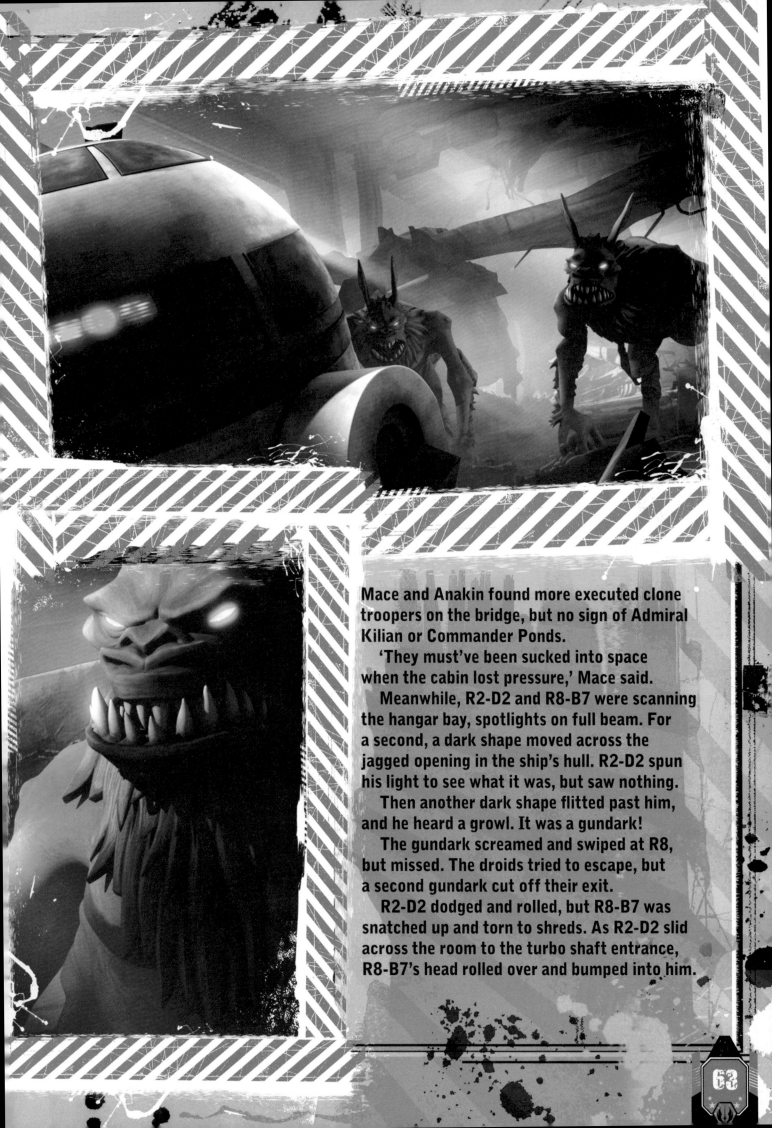

Mace and Anakin found more executed clone troopers on the bridge, but no sign of Admiral Kilian or Commander Ponds.

'They must've been sucked into space when the cabin lost pressure,' Mace said.

Meanwhile, R2-D2 and R8-B7 were scanning the hangar bay, spotlights on full beam. For a second, a dark shape moved across the jagged opening in the ship's hull. R2-D2 spun his light to see what it was, but saw nothing.

Then another dark shape flitted past him, and he heard a growl. It was a gundark!

The gundark screamed and swiped at R8, but missed. The droids tried to escape, but a second gundark cut off their exit.

R2-D2 dodged and rolled, but R8-B7 was snatched up and torn to shreds. As R2-D2 slid across the room to the turbo shaft entrance, R8-B7's head rolled over and bumped into him.

Anakin spotted something on the bridge gangway.

'Is that a Mandalorian helmet?' he asked, walking towards it.

Mace recognised the helmet. 'Clone cadets,' he murmured to himself. 'Jango Fett... Boba...'

As Anakin knelt down beside the helmet, the pieces of the puzzle came together in Mace's mind. Boba Fett had been one of the clone cadets aboard the *Endurance*, determined to destroy the Jedi who had killed his father!

'ANAKIN, NO!' he yelled.

But Anakin picked up the helmet.

BOOOOMMM!

The blast rocked the ship and down in the hangar the gundarks ran to escape the explosion, leaving R2-D2 in one piece.

From a clifftop in the distance, the explosion looked like a blossoming flower. The watching bounty hunters exchanged glances.

'I don't think he's dead,' said Boba.

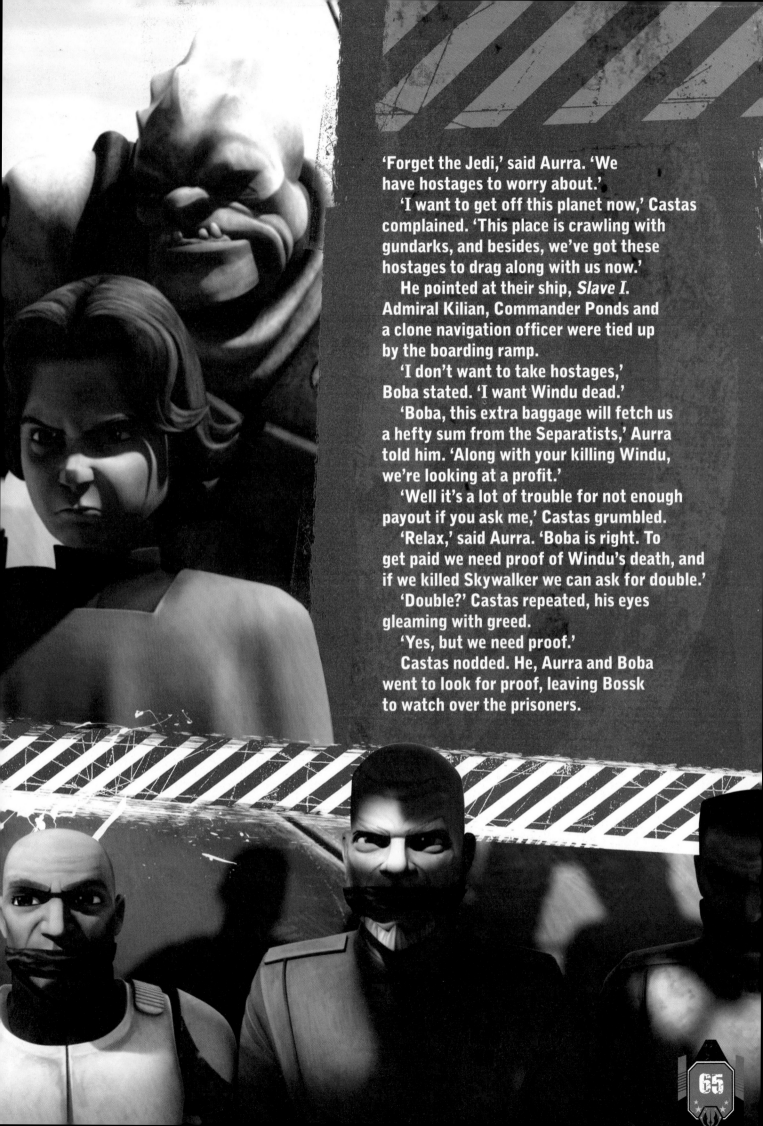

'Forget the Jedi,' said Aurra. 'We have hostages to worry about.'

'I want to get off this planet now,' Castas complained. 'This place is crawling with gundarks, and besides, we've got these hostages to drag along with us now.'

He pointed at their ship, *Slave I*. Admiral Kilian, Commander Ponds and a clone navigation officer were tied up by the boarding ramp.

'I don't want to take hostages,' Boba stated. 'I want Windu dead.'

'Boba, this extra baggage will fetch us a hefty sum from the Separatists,' Aurra told him. 'Along with your killing Windu, we're looking at a profit.'

'Well it's a lot of trouble for not enough payout if you ask me,' Castas grumbled.

'Relax,' said Aurra. 'Boba is right. To get paid we need proof of Windu's death, and if we killed Skywalker we can ask for double.'

'Double?' Castas repeated, his eyes gleaming with greed.

'Yes, but we need proof.'

Castas nodded. He, Aurra and Boba went to look for proof, leaving Bossk to watch over the prisoners.

R2-D2 rocketed up to the shattered bridge. He found Anakin pinned under heavy debris. 'Good to see you, buddy,' said Anakin weakly. R2-D2 tried to clear some of the wreckage, and found Mace, who had been knocked out.

Frantic to save his masters, the little droid dug into the debris. More rubble began to move and fall.

'Careful, Artoo!' Anakin said, coughing feebly. 'I'm afraid the whole bridge will collapse. I need you to go back to the fighters and call the Temple for help, okay?'

R2-D2 beeped in agreement. Then he spotted the bounty hunter speeder bikes approaching and warned Anakin.

'You're going to have to handle this one,' Anakin told him. 'Cut them off somehow, then go get help. We'll hold out as long as we can. Go on, Artoo, go on!'

R2-D2 beeped and rocketed away.

Castas, Aurra and Boba pulled up on their speeder bikes and started to pick their way into the ruins of the *Endurance*.

'Come on,' said Boba. 'We've got to find Windu's body.'

'Careful Boba!' Aurra called.

As Boba walked forwards, a large piece of debris crashed down and almost hit him. He leaped out of the way.

'Yeah, careful,' said Castas with deep sarcasm. 'I'd hate to only split the money three ways.'

They scowled at each other and clambered through the rubble, not guessing that a little droid was watching them. R2-D2 pushed a large piece of metal and sent it crashing down on them.

The bounty hunters only just got out of the way in time.

'This place is a death trap!' said Castas.

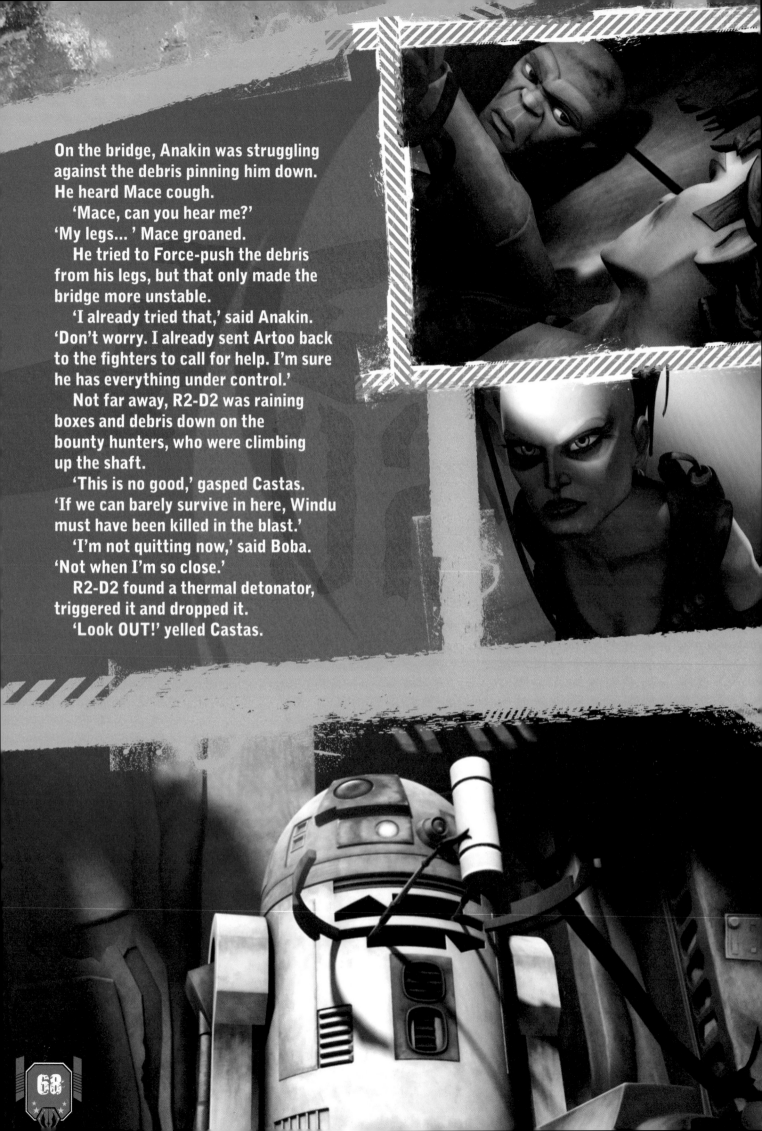

On the bridge, Anakin was struggling against the debris pinning him down. He heard Mace cough.

'Mace, can you hear me?'

'My legs... ' Mace groaned.

He tried to Force-push the debris from his legs, but that only made the bridge more unstable.

'I already tried that,' said Anakin. 'Don't worry. I already sent Artoo back to the fighters to call for help. I'm sure he has everything under control.'

Not far away, R2-D2 was raining boxes and debris down on the bounty hunters, who were climbing up the shaft.

'This is no good,' gasped Castas. 'If we can barely survive in here, Windu must have been killed in the blast.'

'I'm not quitting now,' said Boba. 'Not when I'm so close.'

R2-D2 found a thermal detonator, triggered it and dropped it.

'Look OUT!' yelled Castas.

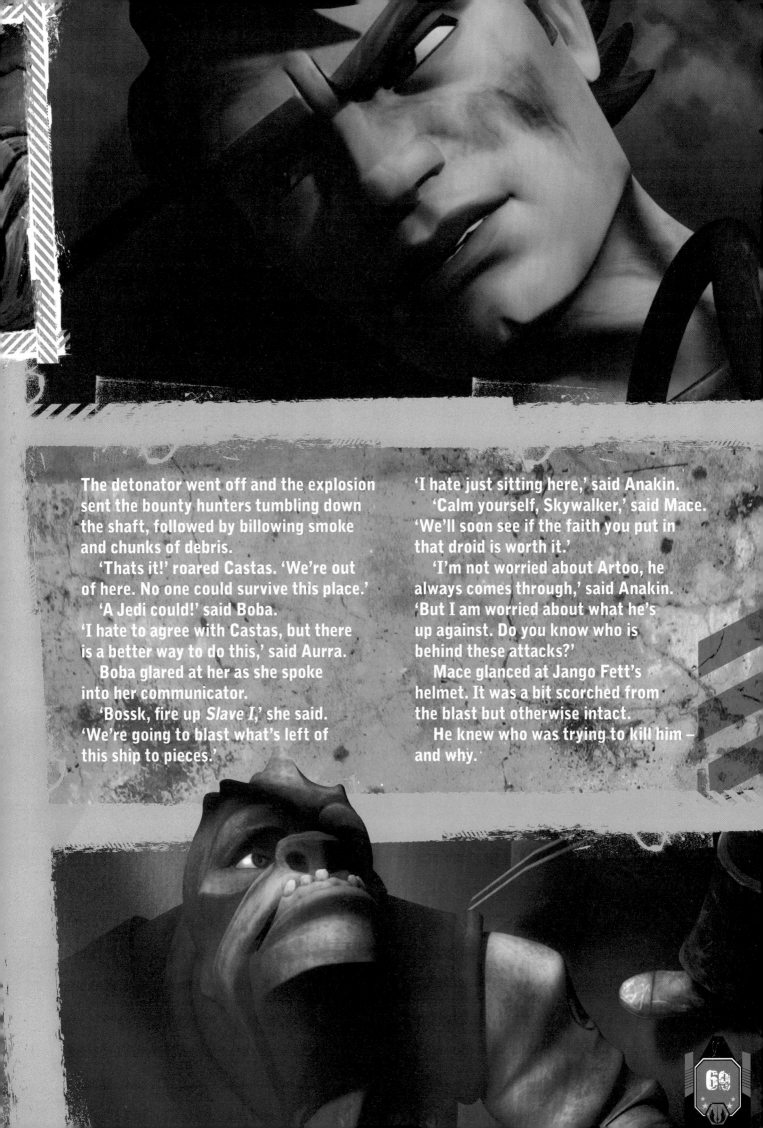

The detonator went off and the explosion sent the bounty hunters tumbling down the shaft, followed by billowing smoke and chunks of debris.

'Thats it!' roared Castas. 'We're out of here. No one could survive this place.'

'A Jedi could!' said Boba.
'I hate to agree with Castas, but there is a better way to do this,' said Aurra.

Boba glared at her as she spoke into her communicator.

'Bossk, fire up *Slave I*,' she said. 'We're going to blast what's left of this ship to pieces.'

'I hate just sitting here,' said Anakin.

'Calm yourself, Skywalker,' said Mace. 'We'll soon see if the faith you put in that droid is worth it.'

'I'm not worried about Artoo, he always comes through,' said Anakin. 'But I am worried about what he's up against. Do you know who is behind these attacks?'

Mace glanced at Jango Fett's helmet. It was a bit scorched from the blast but otherwise intact.

He knew who was trying to kill him – and why.

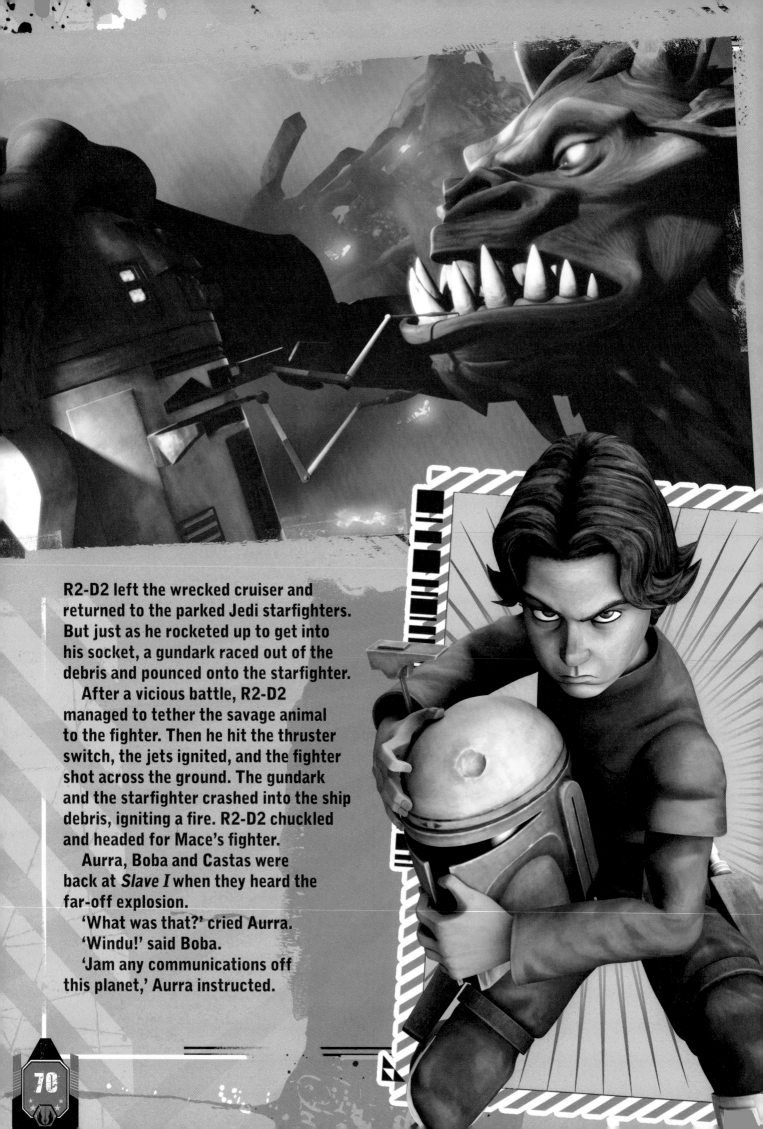

R2-D2 left the wrecked cruiser and returned to the parked Jedi starfighters. But just as he rocketed up to get into his socket, a gundark raced out of the debris and pounced onto the starfighter.

After a vicious battle, R2-D2 managed to tether the savage animal to the fighter. Then he hit the thruster switch, the jets ignited, and the fighter shot across the ground. The gundark and the starfighter crashed into the ship debris, igniting a fire. R2-D2 chuckled and headed for Mace's fighter.

Aurra, Boba and Castas were back at *Slave I* when they heard the far-off explosion.

'What was that?' cried Aurra.

'Windu!' said Boba.

'Jam any communications off this planet,' Aurra instructed.

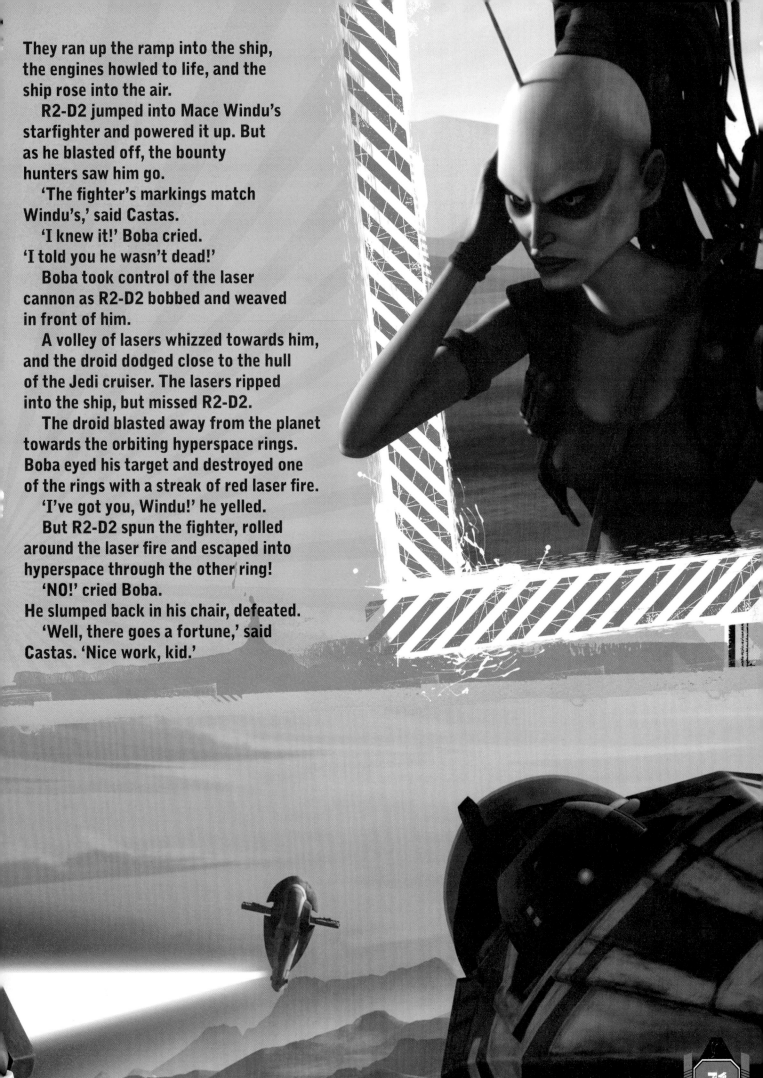

They ran up the ramp into the ship, the engines howled to life, and the ship rose into the air.

R2-D2 jumped into Mace Windu's starfighter and powered it up. But as he blasted off, the bounty hunters saw him go.

'The fighter's markings match Windu's,' said Castas.

'I knew it!' Boba cried. 'I told you he wasn't dead!'

Boba took control of the laser cannon as R2-D2 bobbed and weaved in front of him.

A volley of lasers whizzed towards him, and the droid dodged close to the hull of the Jedi cruiser. The lasers ripped into the ship, but missed R2-D2.

The droid blasted away from the planet towards the orbiting hyperspace rings. Boba eyed his target and destroyed one of the rings with a streak of red laser fire.

'I've got you, Windu!' he yelled.

But R2-D2 spun the fighter, rolled around the laser fire and escaped into hyperspace through the other ring!

'NO!' cried Boba. He slumped back in his chair, defeated.

'Well, there goes a fortune,' said Castas. 'Nice work, kid.'

On the bridge, Mace Force-pulled Jango's helmet to him.

'Whose helmet is that, anyway?' asked Anakin. Mace stared at his reflection in the visor.

'It belongs to a bounty hunter I killed on Geonosis,' he said. 'By the name of Jango Fett.'

'You mean the clone template?' exclaimed Anakin.

'Yes,' said Mace grimly. 'He had a son, or at least a clone he regarded as a son. His name is Boba Fett.'

'I remember now,' said Anakin. 'Obi-Wan listed him in his report on Kamino.'

'Boba was on Geonosis when his father died,' Mace went on. 'He watched as I killed him.'

'That would complicate things,' Anakin said.

'Indeed.'

Aboard Slave I, the bounty hunters were furious.

'This has gone well,' Castas was growling. 'Windu will be back here with a fleet. He'll hunt us down!'

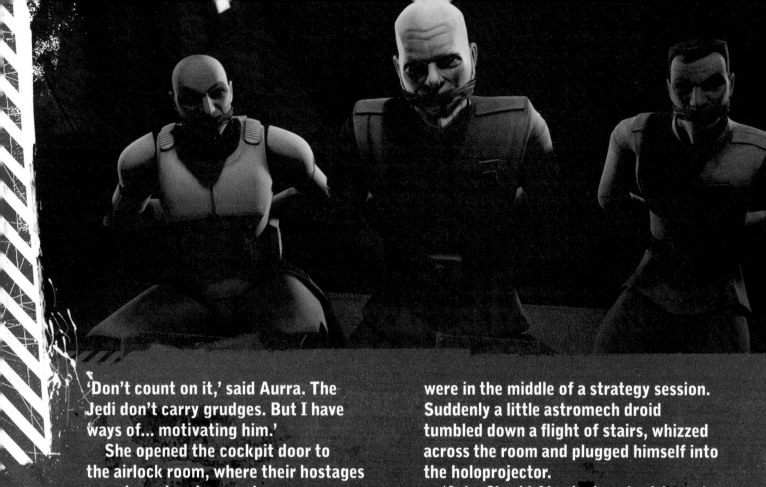

'Don't count on it,' said Aurra. The Jedi don't carry grudges. But I have ways of... motivating him.'

She opened the cockpit door to the airlock room, where their hostages were bound and gagged.

'We'll make Windu come to us next time, on our terms,' Aurra went on. 'Now, lets get out of here. I want to regroup.'

Boba stared at the hostages as Slave I left the planet.

In the War Room of the Jedi Temple on Coruscant, a roomful of senior Jedi were in the middle of a strategy session. Suddenly a little astromech droid tumbled down a flight of stairs, whizzed across the room and plugged himself into the holoprojector.

'Artoo?' said Ahsoka in astonishment. 'What's wrong?'

'You know this droid?' asked Plo Koon.

'It's Anakin's droid, Artoo Detoo,' Ahsoka explained.

Plo Koon nodded. 'Well then, Artoo, deliver the message you so obviously need to communicate.'

In the remains of the *Endurance*, Mace and Anakin were in trouble. The explosion that R2-D2 had caused was threatening what was left of the ship. The engines were on fire and small explosions were happening all over the wreck.

The Jedi had built a makeshift barrier betw... ...es and the approaching fla... ...th... clothes were start...

'Your... gone to...

...come through,' ...d.

...too much trust in ...droid,' Mace replied.

The bridge trembled and began to collapse. Just then, three of Plo Koon's gunships appeared around the collapsing bridge. They were saved in the nick of time!

A short while later, Ahsoka and Plo Koon tended to Anakin and Mace, who were lying on hoversleds.

'Some pretty serious burns,' said Ahsoka, 'but nothing a night in the bacta-tank won't fix.'

She patted her Master on the shoulder and he winced.

'We were lucky to arrive when we did,' said Plo Koon.

'Guess we have Artoo to thank for that,' Ahsoka added.

Mace looked sternly at the little astromech.

'Come here, droid,' he said.

R2-D2 gave a few nervous beeps as he approached.

'I can see why your Master trusts you, little one,' Mace said. 'Good job.'

R2-D2 gave a series of happy beeps.

'That's definitely more praise than I ever get!' said Anakin with a grin.

PINPOINT THE PODS

Following an explosion on the mighty cruiser *Endurance*, escape pods have been scattered in orbit over Vanquor. Help the Republic frigate to gather them in by recording how many escape pods of each colour you can see.

7 RED ESCAPE PODS   **8** YELLOW ESCAPE PODS   **6** GREEN ESCAPE PODS   **6** BLUE ESCAPE PODS

DANGER IN THE SHADOWS

Look at these menacing silhouettes. Can you identify to whom each one belongs?

77

BOBA FETT

Boba Fett is a genetic copy of the bounty hunter Jango Fett. He was born in the cloning facilities of Tipoca City on the planet of Kamino, and he looks exactly the same as the thousands of other clones grown by the Kaminoans.

Genetically he is very different from them. At Jango's request, Boba's genetic structure was not altered, accelerated or weakened.

Boba loved his father, Jango, very much. He has fond memories of their quiet, happy life on Kamino, learning survival and martial skills or just fishing for rollerfish. He was taught to read by Zam Wesell, a Clawdite.

After Zam's death, Jango gave Boba a message unit shaped like a black book. Jango said that if anything ever happened to him, the

black book would give Boba instructions on how to survive.

His happy life changed forever when Obi-Wan Kenobi came to Kamino.

The Fetts fled to Geonosis, where a battle broke out between the Jedi and the Separatists. Jango was killed by Mace Windu, and Boba saw everything. He clutched Jango's Mandalorian helmet in grief and despair as the battle raged around him.

After Jango's death, Boba's hatred of the Jedi knew no bounds. He flew his ship *Slave I* to Kamino to retrieve the message unit left by his father.

After many adventures, Boba has teamed up with Aurra Sing, a bounty hunter who hates the Jedi with equal passion. Slowly, the boy's happy memories are being buried under a shell of vengeful thoughts and hatred.

Naming Ceremony

First name:
Bhaya

Last name:
Nis-notsku

Place of birth:
Northampton

First pet:
Fish Flussy

Last car you were in:
Nissan

To get your Jedi first name

1 Write down the first three letters of your last name.

2 Add the first two letters of your first name.

To get your Jedi last name

1 Write down the first three letters of the last car you were in.

2 Insert a dash.

3 Write down the last three letters of your place of birth in reverse order.

4 Add the first three letters of your first pet.

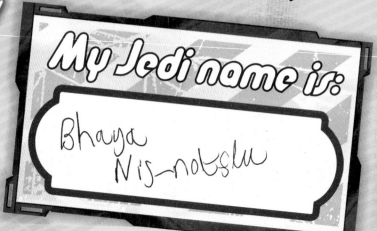

My Jedi name is:

Bhaya
Nis-notsku

WEEQUAY WANTED!

These Weequay pirates are wanted for crimes across the galaxy. Use your colouring pens to complete this Wanted poster.

CHRISTMAS CLONES

FOLLOW THESE SIMPLE INSTRUCTIONS TO CREATE AWESOME CLONE CHRISTMAS TREE DECORATIONS!

You will need:
Black felt
Grey or silver felt
Needle and grey thread
Silver ribbon • Fabric glue
Cotton wool
Scissors

1 Cut two clone trooper body shapes from grey or silver felt, using the template to help you.

2 Cut a length of ribbon and put the ends between the two felt bodies. (The ribbon will hang from the top of the head, and you can use it to hang the decoration on your tree.)

3 Ask an adult to help you sew the bodies together, holding the ribbon in place. Leave a small gap, which you will use to stuff the decoration.

4 Fill the decoration with cotton wool (not too full) and then sew the gap closed.

5 To make the visor and gloves, cut the shapes from the black felt and glue them in place.

6 As soon as the glue is dry, hang the decoration on your Christmas tree.

Be careful
with scissors!
Ask an adult
to help.

Wordsearch

Inside this grid are some of the most famous and infamous names of the Clone Wars. Can you find them all?

```
C Y T O N T D O I S N H Y T E R P I A I
I C A T A Y W Z R I O P A S U F T B D M
T O Y I F Q D I J X L P H W A I Y E O N
S E N C U G N U N A L T S W U B X P Y S
H A P N E L A K A N H O O D N O H C R N
P A L P A T I N E A R S K A L N B Y A C
A D O F R E I F U K A K A S D E T L E D
D I K A O E R R H I I T T T E K A I T A
M S O N W Y R T Y N N C A E S N D N K T
E H O O A A T O S S L H N U T A I M B I
A E N T S I P R D K E I O E N W C D U I
M Q A I V E M I F Y U E T S E I S E U A
I G N M G P A S T W I N S E N B U H O I
D G D D I E C T H A G S N W I O O D L L
A I P G E N E R A L G R I E V O U S L A
L B O Y D F W S T K Y P T A P H R O S R
A H D A A W I E A E I W A O M U A H T K
B E S B R H N A C R W C L U S E W C R N
O N O A O D D S N A I S O D N H I T A J
P B I S Y E U Y U E U K O O D T N U O C
```

 GENERAL GRIEVOUS

AHSOKA TANO

 ANAKIN SKYWALKER

 **AURRA SING**

BOBA FETT

BOSSK

CASTAS

 **COUNT DOOKU**

HONDO OHNAKA

MACE WINDU

OBI-WAN KENOBI

PADMÉ AMIDALA

PALPATINE

PLO KOON

 YODA

True or False?

Have you been paying attention to the story so far? Answer these pop quiz questions to find out.

1. The *Endurance* is a shuttlecraft. ⬡

2. Whiplash and Hotrod are faithful Republican droids. ⬡

3. Aurra Sing has chalk-white skin. ⬡

4. Jax is a Clone Commander. ⬡

5. Anakin killed Boba Fett's mother. ⬡

6. A Republic medical frigate explodes the scattered escape pods. ⬡

7. Anakin and Mace get trapped inside the wreckage of the *Millennium Falcon*. ⬡

8. Boba owns a Mandalorian helmet. ⬡

9. Embo is a member of Aurra Sing's bounty hunter gang. ⬡

10. The bounty hunters murder Admiral Kilian. ⬡

11. Anakin and Mace rescue three stranded clone cadets. ⬡

12. Bossk is a smelly bounty hunter. ⬡

13. The clone cadets stay on board the damaged Jedi cruiser. ⬡

14. Mace Windu killed the genetic original of the clone troopers. ⬡

15. Castas is a Togruta warrior. ⬡

1-8
Very poor. Go back and read the story again!

9-12
Quite good, but your attention could be better.

13-15
Excellent!

85

IN-DEPTH PROFILE: AURRA SING

Aurra Sing is a ruthless bounty hunter who despises the Jedi Order. However, she once trained under the Dark Woman, the Jedi Master who first identified Ki-Adi-Mundi as a Jedi hopeful.

The Jedi Council hoped that the Dark Woman would bond with the girl, but Aurra was a difficult, stubborn student. She had a cunning instinct and deadly reflexes, but lacked the control to fully master the Force. Eventually she failed her training and used her abilities to become a bounty hunter instead.

Aurra enjoyed her dangerous life, because it gave her a focus for her aggression. She learned martial arts and hunting skills. When a Hutt crime lord captured her and apprenticed her to a group of cruel Anzati, her abilities were honed and perfected. Under their instruction, Aurra lost all

traces of compassion. She became a deadly killer, seeking revenge on all who had wronged her in the past.

She is now a frighteningly efficient assassin who specializes in Jedi hunts. She carries a trophy case with several lightsabers as a testament to her abilities. Aurra gets great personal satisfaction from stalking Force-sensitive prey.

Weapons

Aurra uses a variety of tools during her hunts, including electrobinoculars, vibroblades, projectile rifles, standard blasters, a portable scanner, a jetpack and a ryyk blade. She also employs the Force as a weapon, using her mind powers to take control of her enemies. A long, thin Rhen-Orm biocomputer antenna is surgically attached to her skull.

VITAL STATISTICS

Homeworld: Nar Shaddaa
Species: Unknown
Gender: Female
Size: 1.74 metres
Weapon: Lightsaber, projectile rifle, blasters
Vehicle: Modified swoop
Affiliation: Bounty hunter, former Jedi

THE CLONE WARS™

✦ LETHAL TRACKDOWN

Slave I darted through the vastness of the void, carrying the bounty hunters and their hostages. Boba Fett had already made two failed attempts on Mace Windu's life.

Now Boba's mentor, Aurra Sing, had taken three Republic officers hostage to force Windu to face Boba on their terms. However, Boba didn't like the way things were working out. When he spoke to the hostages, Admiral Kilian sensed his doubts.

'You don't have to do this,' said Kilian. 'You're not like them. I can tell.'

'What do you know, old man?' Boba snapped.

'I know a good soldier when I see one.' But Boba did not want to hear this.

'I'm no soldier,' he stated. 'I'm no clone, not like those two!'

Mace Windu and Anakin Skywalker were resting in the Jedi Temple medical bay.

'What are you planning to do with this son of Jango Fett?' Anakin asked, staring out of the window.

'I am not planning to do anything,' said Mace.

Anakin turned to him in surprise. 'That kid destroyed an entire cruiser trying to get you, and you're just going to let it go?'

'Is there something else I should be doing, Skywalker?' Mace asked mildly.

'How about tracking him down?' asked Anakin.

Mace looked up at him. 'So I should behave as this child does? I should seek revenge?'

'No not revenge, Master,' said Anakin. 'A pre-emptive strike. He's going to kill you!'

Just then, Ahsoka entered the room with Jedi Master Plo Koon.

'We received a transmission from the bounty hunters,' said Plo. 'They apparently took hostages.'

Plo showed them the hologram of Aurra Sing, Boba and the hostages.

'Mace Windu!' Boba said. 'You were lucky to escape. Your friends here were not so fortunate.'

The shocked Jedi recognised the crew of Mace's destroyed Jedi cruiser, *Endurance.*

'Until you face Boba, these men will be killed one at a time,' said Aurra, moving over to one of the clone hostages. 'Boba, do it.'

Boba's gun wavered and he pulled it back. He couldn't do it, but Aurra did not have such tender feelings. She shot Commander Ponds dead.

'Only two to go, Windu,' she said. 'Come and find us. We'll be waiting!'

The hologram ended and the Jedi were quiet for a moment.

'I'll go,' said Mace, breaking the silence.

'You are not ready to travel and your presence would only aggravate the boy,' said Plo. 'I will go, and take Padawan Tano with me.'

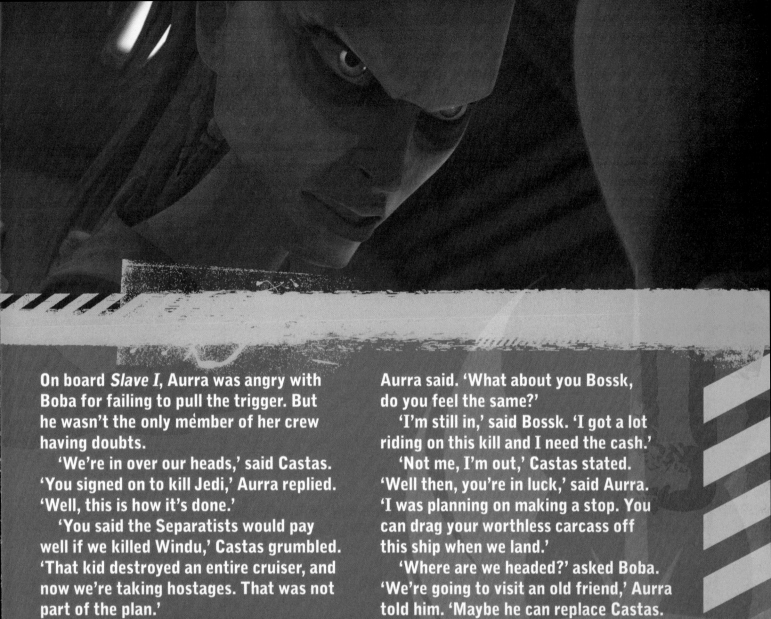

On board *Slave I*, Aurra was angry with Boba for failing to pull the trigger. But he wasn't the only member of her crew having doubts.

'We're in over our heads,' said Castas. 'You signed on to kill Jedi,' Aurra replied. 'Well, this is how it's done.'

'You said the Separatists would pay well if we killed Windu,' Castas grumbled. 'That kid destroyed an entire cruiser, and now we're taking hostages. That was not part of the plan.'

'I never took you for a coward, Castas,' Aurra said. 'What about you Bossk, do you feel the same?'

'I'm still in,' said Bossk. 'I got a lot riding on this kill and I need the cash.'

'Not me, I'm out,' Castas stated. 'Well then, you're in luck,' said Aurra. 'I was planning on making a stop. You can drag your worthless carcass off this ship when we land.'

'Where are we headed?' asked Boba. 'We're going to visit an old friend,' Aurra told him. 'Maybe he can replace Castas. Set course for Florrum.'

On Florrum, Aurra headed for Hondo Ohnaka's pirate stronghold. They were old friends, and Hondo looked at Boba questioningly.

'Part of my crew,' Aurra explained. 'He's Jango's son.'

'Ah yes, sorry about your father,' Hondo said to Boba. 'He was a friend and an honourable man.'

'And that's Castas,' Aurra continued. 'But he's getting off here.'

She looked scornfully at the Klatooinian, who glared back at her.

Hondo invited them to his compound bar and ordered drinks. Castas headed over to a holo transmitter to make a call. Aurra didn't follow him, but she raised her head antenna so that she could overhear his conversation.

'I'm stuck out here on Florrum,' Castas was saying to his friend Fong Do, another bounty hunter.

'I warned you,' said Fong Do. 'Working with Aurra Sing is bad business.'

'This job's gone south,' Castas complained. 'I have some information. Information that's worth something to the right people.'

'What kind of people?' asked Fong Do.

'That's where you come in,' said Castas.

He was going to betray Aurra, and she couldn't allow that. She drew her blaster pistol and shot Castas straight through the chest.

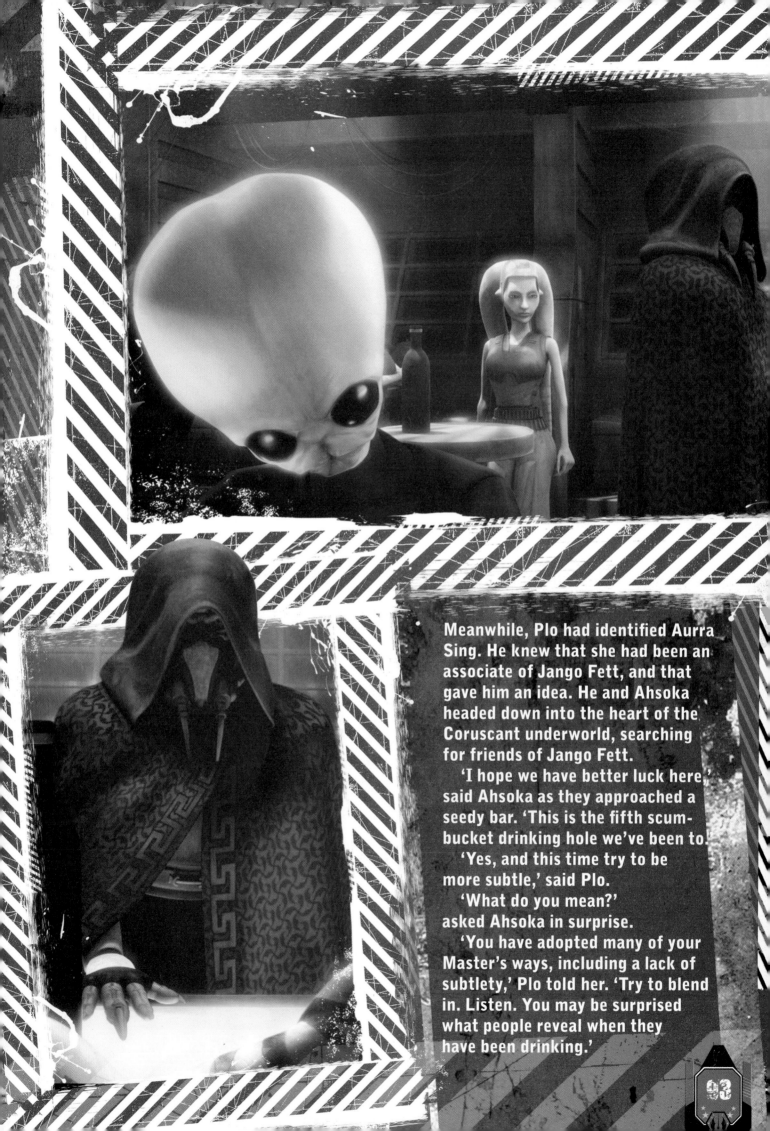

Meanwhile, Plo had identified Aurra Sing. He knew that she had been an associate of Jango Fett, and that gave him an idea. He and Ahsoka headed down into the heart of the Coruscant underworld, searching for friends of Jango Fett.

'I hope we have better luck here,' said Ahsoka as they approached a seedy bar. 'This is the fifth scum-bucket drinking hole we've been to.'

'Yes, and this time try to be more subtle,' said Plo.

'What do you mean?' asked Ahsoka in surprise.

'You have adopted many of your Master's ways, including a lack of subtlety,' Plo told her. 'Try to blend in. Listen. You may be surprised what people reveal when they have been drinking.'

The bar was illuminated by a strange, orange light. Ahsoka looked around while Plo spoke to the bartender.

'I need some information,' he said. 'We're not sellin' that here, pal,' said the bartender.

Plo moved his poncho aside so the bartender could see his lightsaber.

'Been a while since we had one of you down here,' said the bartender cautiously. 'Aren't you a bit busy with your war to be botherin' with the likes of us?'

'We are never too busy for the citizens of the Republic,' said Plo. 'Now, tell me, do you know the whereabouts of Aurra Sing?'

Ahsoka was walking past tables of thugs, listening to their conversations as she went. She saw a bounty hunter laughing with some Weequay pirates and moved closer. 'Florrum?' the bounty hunter was saying. 'A buddy of mine was just murdered on Florrum.'

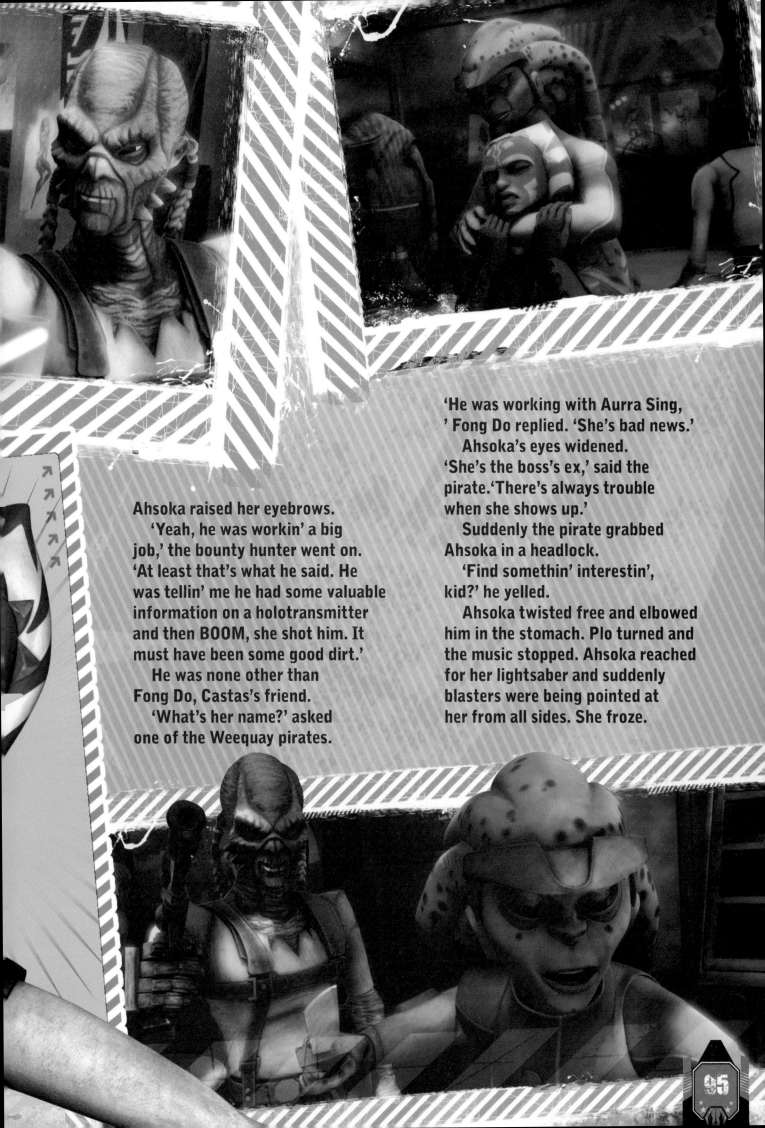

Ahsoka raised her eyebrows.
'Yeah, he was workin' a big job,' the bounty hunter went on. 'At least that's what he said. He was tellin' me he had some valuable information on a holotransmitter and then BOOM, she shot him. It must have been some good dirt.'

He was none other than Fong Do, Castas's friend.

'What's her name?' asked one of the Weequay pirates.

'He was working with Aurra Sing, ' Fong Do replied. 'She's bad news.'

Ahsoka's eyes widened.

'She's the boss's ex,' said the pirate. 'There's always trouble when she shows up.'

Suddenly the pirate grabbed Ahsoka in a headlock.

'Find somethin' interestin', kid?' he yelled.

Ahsoka twisted free and elbowed him in the stomach. Plo turned and the music stopped. Ahsoka reached for her lightsaber and suddenly blasters were being pointed at her from all sides. She froze.

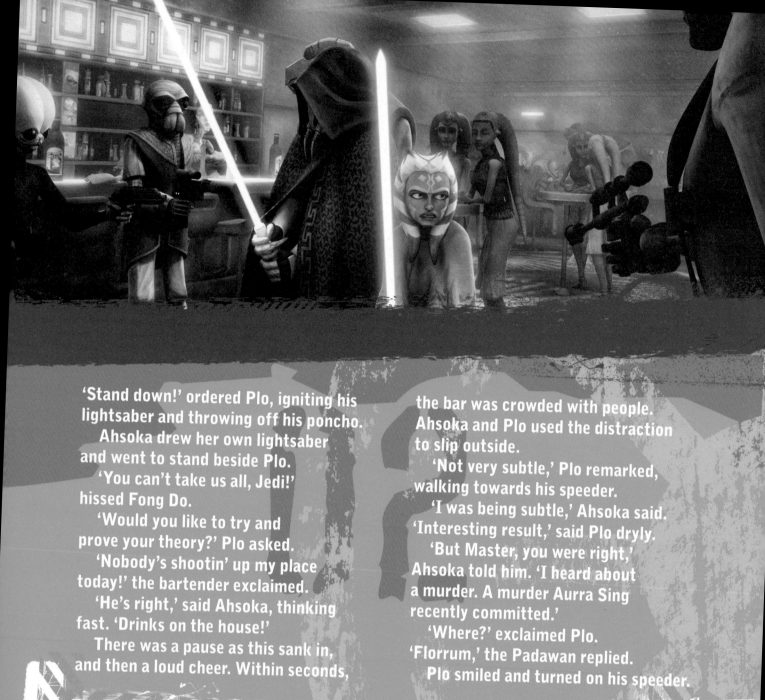

'Stand down!' ordered Plo, igniting his lightsaber and throwing off his poncho.

Ahsoka drew her own lightsaber and went to stand beside Plo.

'You can't take us all, Jedi!' hissed Fong Do.

'Would you like to try and prove your theory?' Plo asked.

'Nobody's shootin' up my place today!' the bartender exclaimed.

'He's right,' said Ahsoka, thinking fast. 'Drinks on the house!'

There was a pause as this sank in, and then a loud cheer. Within seconds, the bar was crowded with people. Ahsoka and Plo used the distraction to slip outside.

'Not very subtle,' Plo remarked, walking towards his speeder.

'I was being subtle,' Ahsoka said. 'Interesting result,' said Plo dryly.

'But Master, you were right,' Ahsoka told him. 'I heard about a murder. A murder Aurra Sing recently committed.'

'Where?' exclaimed Plo. 'Florrum,' the Padawan replied. Plo smiled and turned on his speeder.

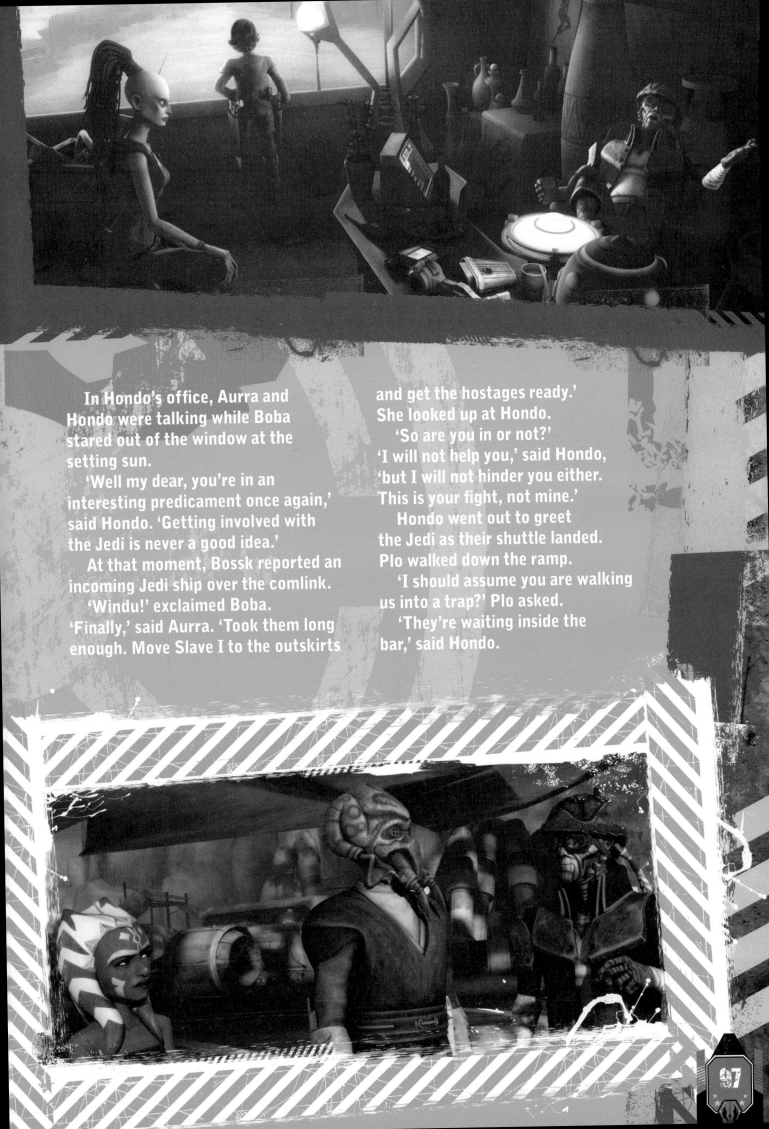

In Hondo's office, Aurra and Hondo were talking while Boba stared out of the window at the setting sun.

'Well my dear, you're in an interesting predicament once again,' said Hondo. 'Getting involved with the Jedi is never a good idea.'

At that moment, Bossk reported an incoming Jedi ship over the comlink.

'Windu!' exclaimed Boba.

'Finally,' said Aurra. 'Took them long enough. Move Slave I to the outskirts and get the hostages ready.' She looked up at Hondo.

'So are you in or not?'

'I will not help you,' said Hondo, 'but I will not hinder you either. This is your fight, not mine.'

Hondo went out to greet the Jedi as their shuttle landed. Plo walked down the ramp.

'I should assume you are walking us into a trap?' Plo asked.

'They're waiting inside the bar,' said Hondo.

The bar was empty except for Aurra. She was sitting at a table in a pool of light. Plo sat down opposite her.

'Bad move, Jedi,' she said. 'This will cost you.'

Boba stepped out of the shadows and aimed a gun at Plo's head.

'I wanted Windu,' he said. 'What are you doing here?'

'We can do this the difficult way, or the simple way,' said Plo. 'The choice is yours.'

Aurra sneered at Plo, her head antenna rising.

'Bossk, can you hear me?' she asked.

Antenna static crackled as Bossk responded.

'Roger.'

'Execute the hostages if I give the word,' she ordered.

'Unwise,' said Plo. 'You have already lost and you don't even know it.'

A shadowy figure moved across the bar, but Aurra didn't seem to notice.

'I am prepared to kill you, the hostages, whatever it takes to get what Boba wants,' she said.

'It sounds more like what you want,' Plo remarked.

As fast as lightning, Ahsoka stepped out of the shadows behind Aurra and cut off the bounty hunter's antenna. She held her lightsaber to Aurra's throat, and Boba moved his gun closer to Plo.

'Let her go,' he said.

'No chance,' said Ahsoka.

'She won't do it, Boba,' Aurra exclaimed. 'She's not like you!'

'She's right,' said Ahsoka. 'I'm not a murderer.'

'I'm not a murderer, but I want justice!' Boba cried.

'We are justice,' said Plo. Boba hesitated and looked at Aurra.

'Don't listen to them,' she urged him. 'No one will be harmed if you come quietly,' Plo promised.

'I can't let you die,' Boba said to Aurra.

'You won't have to,' she replied. She lifted her boot, which was fitted with toe darts, and winked at Boba. Then things started to happen very quickly.

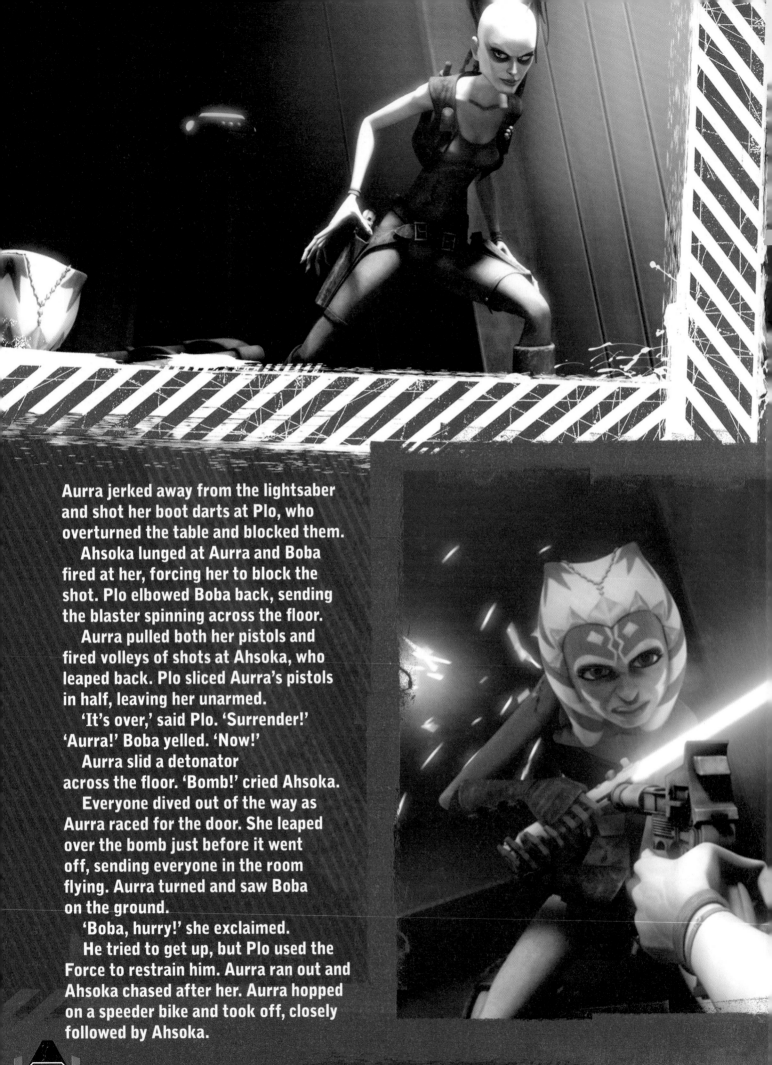

Aurra jerked away from the lightsaber and shot her boot darts at Plo, who overturned the table and blocked them.

Ahsoka lunged at Aurra and Boba fired at her, forcing her to block the shot. Plo elbowed Boba back, sending the blaster spinning across the floor.

Aurra pulled both her pistols and fired volleys of shots at Ahsoka, who leaped back. Plo sliced Aurra's pistols in half, leaving her unarmed.

'It's over,' said Plo. 'Surrender!'
'Aurra!' Boba yelled. 'Now!'

Aurra slid a detonator across the floor. 'Bomb!' cried Ahsoka.

Everyone dived out of the way as Aurra raced for the door. She leaped over the bomb just before it went off, sending everyone in the room flying. Aurra turned and saw Boba on the ground.

'Boba, hurry!' she exclaimed.

He tried to get up, but Plo used the Force to restrain him. Aurra ran out and Ahsoka chased after her. Aurra hopped on a speeder bike and took off, closely followed by Ahsoka.

'Aurra, help!' Boba cried. 'Help me! Don't leave me!'

But it was too late – she had gone. 'The hostages, where are they?' Plo demanded. 'Boba, if you don't tell us where those men are they are going to die! Innocent men!'

'She left me,' whispered Boba. Plo handcuffed Boba and led him out of the bar to where Hondo was standing.

'He will not reveal the location of the hostages,' Plo said.

Hondo turned to Boba and saw the sorrow in his eyes.

'Tell the Jedi what he wants to know, Boba,' he said.

'Why should I help anybody?' Boba demanded. 'I've got no one!'

'It is the honourable thing to do,' said Hondo quietly. It's what your father would have wanted.'

Miserably, Boba told Plo where to find the hostages. Plo made contact with Ahsoka and gave her the coordinates.

Bossk was preparing to execute the hostages when a speeder bike screamed into the landing area. He looked up and saw Ahsoka, who fired a volley of lasers at him.

Dropping his gun, he dived for cover, and she took the chance to cut the hostages loose.

Kilian picked up Bossk's gun as Aurra Sing arrived on her bike. She leaped off the bike and sent it crashing into the one Ahsoka had been riding. Everyone dived for cover as the bikes exploded and smoke and debris filled the air.

Aurra ran into *Slave I* and powered up the engines. Ahsoka raced towards the ship as Admiral Kilian held a gun to Bossk's head.
'Don't move,' he said.

The ship began to take off and Ahsoka leaped onto one of the wings. Aurra looked out and saw Ahsoka hanging on.

The bounty hunter turned the ship sharply to one side to try to knock the girl off.

Ahsoka slashed at the wing with her lightsaber, cutting a stabiliser and sending the ship spinning away.

Ahsoka let go and dropped back to ground as *Slave I* spiralled out of control. The ship hit the ground and a massive explosion illuminated the landing area.

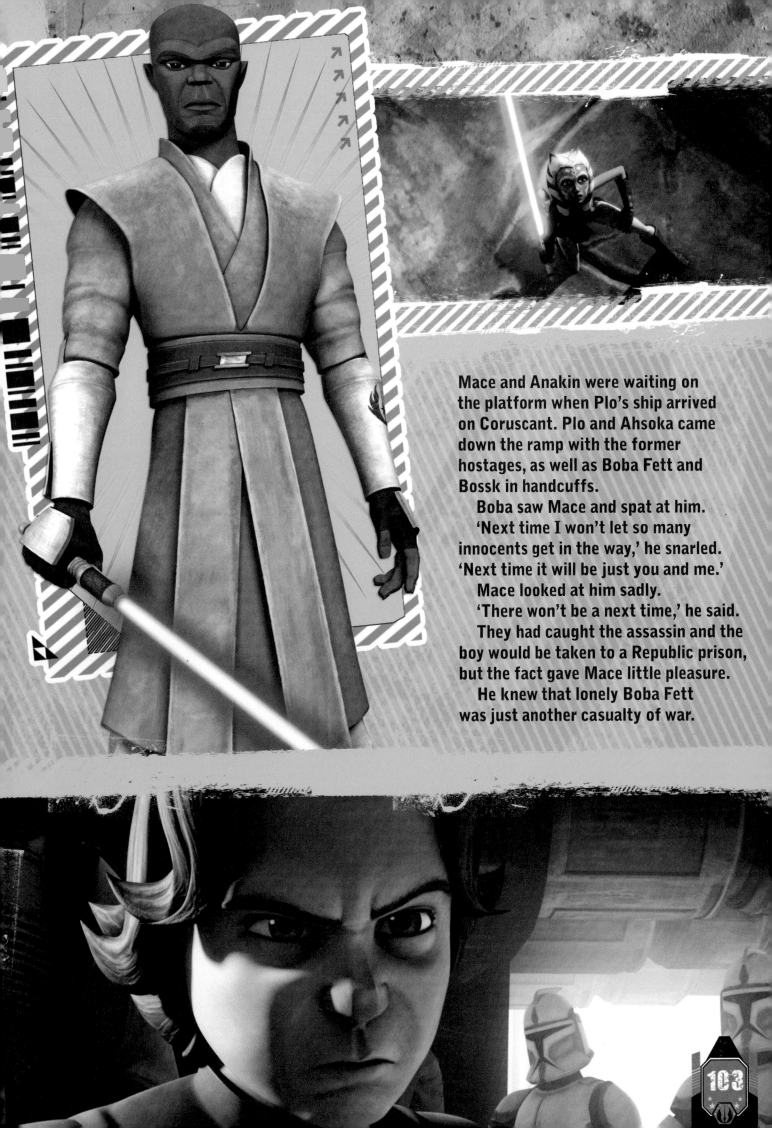

Mace and Anakin were waiting on the platform when Plo's ship arrived on Coruscant. Plo and Ahsoka came down the ramp with the former hostages, as well as Boba Fett and Bossk in handcuffs.

Boba saw Mace and spat at him.

'Next time I won't let so many innocents get in the way,' he snarled. 'Next time it will be just you and me.'

Mace looked at him sadly.

'There won't be a next time,' he said.

They had caught the assassin and the boy would be taken to a Republic prison, but the fact gave Mace little pleasure.

He knew that lonely Boba Fett was just another casualty of war.

Heroes of
the Clone

SPOT THE DIFFERENCE

Look at these two pictures of Boba Fett and his bounty hunter friends. They look the same, but there are ten differences between them. Can you identify all the differences? Circle each one as you find it.

CLONE WARS CROSSWORD

SOLVE THE CLUES AND FILL IN THE CROSSWORD, WORKING DOWNWARDS. THEN REARRANGE THE LETTERS IN THE SHADED SQUARES TO FIND THE NAME OF A BOUNTY HUNTER.

1 Which Jedi Master arrested Bossk and Boba?

2 What is the Chosen One's first name?

3 What is the name of Boba's ship?

4 This pale ex-Jedi's surname rhymes with 'ring'

5 Who sabotaged the Jedi cruiser Endurance?

6 Where is the Jedi Temple?

7 Who was the leader of the bounty hunter gang that defended a Felucian village?

THE HIDDEN BOUNTY HUNTER IS...

Who Dunnit?

Would you make a good sleuth? Look at all these faces, and then read the list of deeds. Draw lines to connect each character with the deed they carried out.

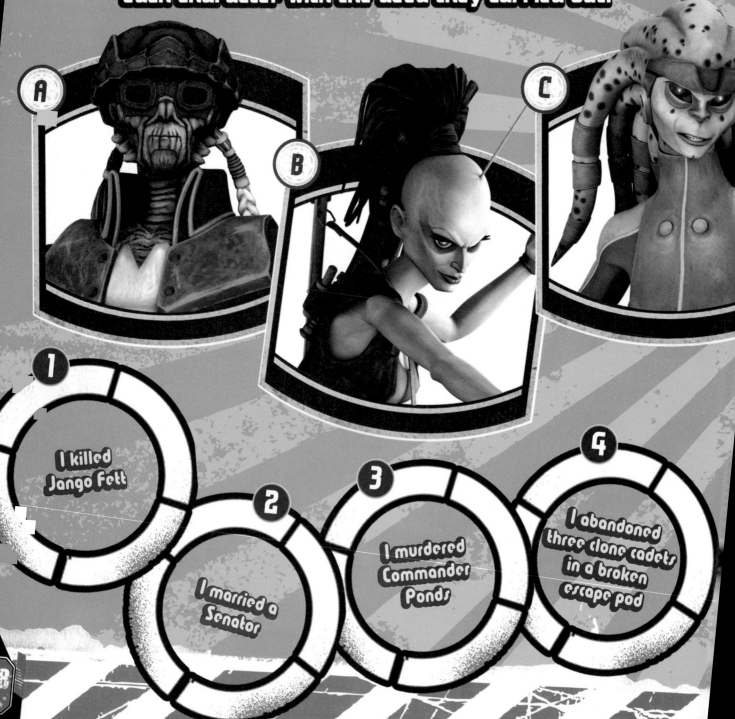

A

B

C

1
I killed Jango Fett

2
I married a Senator

3
I murdered Commander Ponds

4
I abandoned three clone cadets in a broken escape pod

H

G

F

D

E

5
I led an attack on a farming village to take their valuable nysillin

6
I helped to rescue two trapped Jedi from a cruiser

7
I forced a bounty hunter's ship down by cutting a stabiliser

8
I watched a bounty hunter shoot my friend Castas

Answers

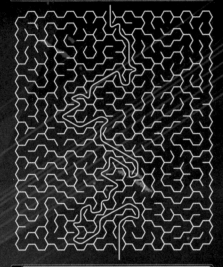

C

1. Padmé Amidala is secretly married to Anakin Skywalker.
2. Anakin Skywalker was once Obi-Wan Kenobi's Padawan.
3. Obi-Wan Kenobi sits on the Jedi Council with Mace Windu, who has a purple lightsaber.
4. Mace Windu killed Jango Fett at the Battle of Geonosis.
5. Jango Fett was the father of Boba Fett.
6. Boba Fett travels the galaxy with a female bounty hunter called Aurra Sing.

3	2	5	8	6	7	9	4	1
6	9	7	4	1	3	2	5	8
8	1	4	5	2	9	7	3	6
7	4	8	9	3	6	1	2	5
2	3	1	7	4	5	6	8	9
5	6	9	1	8	2	3	7	4
9	8	6	3	7	4	5	1	2
1	7	2	6	5	8	4	9	3
4	5	3	2	9	1	8	6	7

1. Ahsoka Tano 2. Hondo Ohnaka
3. Boba Fett 4. Aurra Sing
5. Castas 6. Obi-Wan Kenobi

1. Fake money 2. Breath 3. A river
4. A hole 5. A splinter 6. A cold

6 red pods • 8 yellow pods
7 green pods • 6 blue pods

A) Bossk B) Aurra Sing
C) Castas D) Hondo Ohnaka
E) Count Dooku
F) General Grievous G) Sugi
H) Seripas I) Darth Sidious

1. FALSE 2. FALSE
3. TRUE 4. FALSE
5. FALSE 6. FALSE
7. FALSE 8. TRUE
9. FALSE 10. FALSE
11. TRUE 12. TRUE
13. FALSE 14. TRUE
15. FALSE

The hidden bounty hunter is Serapis.

A. 5 B. 3 C. 8 D. 1 E. 6 F. 7 G. 4 H. 2